24/7

Praise for Yolanda Wallace

The War Within

"*The War Within* has a masterpiece quality to it. It's a story of the heart told with heart—a story to be savored—and proof that you're never too old to find (or rediscover) true love."—*Lambda Literary*

Rum Spring

"The writing was possibly the best I've seen for the modern lesfic genre, and the premise and setting was intriguing. I would recommend this one."—*The Lesbrary*

Murphy's Law

"Prepare to be thrilled by a love story filled with high adventure as they move toward an ending as turbulent as the weather on a Himalayan peak."—*Lambda Literary*

By the Author

In Medias Res

Rum Spring

Lucky Loser

Month of Sundays

Murphy's Law

The War Within

Love's Bounty

Break Point

24/7

Writing as Mason Dixon:

Date with Destiny

Charm City

24/7

by

Yolanda Wallace

2016

24/7

ISBN 13: 978-1-62639-619-7

This Trade Paperback Original Is Published By
Bold Strokes Books, Inc.
P.O. Box 249
Valley Falls, NY 12185

First Edition: March 2016

Credits
Editor: Cindy Cresap
Production Design: Stacia Seaman
Cover Design by Sheri (graphicartist2020@hotmail.com)

Acknowledgments

Most of my books are inspired by conversations that begin with the famous last words, "What if?" This book is no different.

My wife and I were on vacation in Mexico when we noticed the security personnel patrolling the beach next to our resort. Two tequila shots later—okay, maybe three—*24/7* began to take shape.

Travel and food are two of my favorite pastimes. I was able to indulge my love of both while writing this book. I hope you enjoy the journey.

My thanks, as always, to Radclyffe for taking a chance on me when she signed me to my first contract, to Cindy Cresap for making me a better writer one editor's note at a time, and the rest of Team BSB for their hard work and dedication behind the scenes. You rock!

Thank you, Dita, my wife/travel companion/first reader, for always being there whether I feel the need to experiment with a new recipe, plan a trip, or talk through a plot point.

And last but not least, thank you to the readers for your continued support and encouragement. You make the late nights and long weekends worth every second.

To Dita.

Thank you for choosing me as your travel partner.

Vacation Stretcher

Finn Chamberlain settled into her seat at the bar closest to her gate and ordered a Corona, having learned long ago that Mexico's signature beer tasted far better on the north side of the border than it did in its home country. As soon as her plane landed in Cancún, it would be Presidente all the way.

After the bartender placed the beer in front of her, Finn took a long draw from the bottle and checked her watch. Only two more hours before her plane departed Dallas/Fort Worth International Airport for the last of her series of flights. Perhaps one day, she thought with a sigh, she could convince Brett Madison, her editor, to pop for a direct flight instead of one with a slew of connections. But she wasn't holding her breath.

Direct flights were more expensive, and Brett—like most people in charge of the slowly dying medium known as print magazines—liked to keep operating costs low whenever possible. If the circulation numbers didn't start trending upward soon, Finn feared she might find herself strapped to the wing or shoved in the cargo hold instead of sandwiched between two strangers in coach on her next flight. No matter. As long as she got where she was going, she didn't care how long it took to get there or how many "inadvertent" elbows she received from her traveling companions along the way. Being able to tick another country off her bucket list made everything worth it in the end. Usually. The nasty case of dysentery she caught in Mozambique a few years ago had put her theory to a serious test. And the horde of pickpockets in Rio had nearly caused her to lose her faith in humanity. But that was then. This, as they say, was now.

"Is this seat taken?"

Finn looked away from the talking heads on one of the flat-screen TVs mounted above the bar. She tuned out their discussion of the travails of the latest multimillionaire athlete with impulse control issues and turned to face a beautiful Hispanic woman with tawny skin, shining black hair, and the brownest eyes she had ever seen.

"No, it isn't." Finn nudged her backpack and rolling carry-on out of the way with her foot. "Feel free."

"Thanks." The woman straddled the bar stool, dropped a rucksack between her feet, and raised a hand to get the bartender's attention. "I'll have what she's having," she said in slightly accented English before flashing a dimpled grin. "I've always wanted to say that."

"Yeah, me, too." Finn wanted to kick herself for not coming up with something more original, but she felt so tongue-tied she could barely remember how to speak English, let alone form coherent sentences. Wit was too much to ask.

"Maybe next time, eh?"

"Maybe."

Finn turned back to *SportsCenter*, but regarded the woman out of the corner of her eye. The woman was wearing a form-fitting white Henley with the sleeves pushed up to her elbows, revealing wiry but powerful-looking forearms. Her jeans fit her like a second skin, hugging narrow hips and corded thighs. Her black boots and olive rucksack hinted at a military background, but her ramrod-straight posture and squared shoulders truly brought the image home. Finn took another sip of her beer and considered the unlikely possibility that her accidental encounter with her new drinking buddy could be the first of many instead of the once-in-a-lifetime meeting it would probably turn out to be. Nah. No way she could ever get that lucky. Not in this lifetime.

The woman wiped her hand on her jeans and extended it toward Finn. "My name's Luisa. What's yours?"

Finn introduced herself, impressed—and a little aroused—by the firmness of Luisa's handshake. Strong women had always been her weakness. And even though they had just met, she could already tell Luisa was a 5′8″ bundle of kryptonite.

"This may seem like an odd request," she said, "but will you take my picture?"

Finn pulled a miniature Porky Pig figurine from her backpack and offered Luisa her phone.

"Sure," Luisa said curiously. "Who's your friend?"

Finn glanced at the toy in her hand while Luisa lined up her shot. "It seems stupid, I know, but I take him with me on every trip. He has nearly as many passport stamps as I do."

"Is he your mascot or your good luck charm?"

Luisa pressed a button on the phone's display screen. Finn heard an automated click as the camera captured her image.

"A bit of both, I guess. I bought him while I was on spring break during my freshman year of college. We've been hanging out together ever since."

"I've always admired his fashion sense," Luisa said after she returned Finn's phone. "The blazer and bow tie with no pants thing is rather daring, don't you think?"

"Porky's my role model in some things, but not in others." Finn slipped her phone into her back pocket. "When I want fashion tips, I turn to She-Ra. She's a much snappier dresser than Porky. In fact, *Cosmo* once named her one of the fifteen most stylish cartoon characters of all time."

"Nice choice." Luisa openly looked her up and down. "You would look great wearing her breast plate, boots, and arm guards, but I would ditch the headpiece if I were you."

"Point taken."

Finn took a sip of her beer to hide her smile. Luisa not only got her slightly off-kilter sense of humor, she shared it as well. Finn couldn't remember the last time she had felt such an immediate kinship with someone. A coupling that felt right in every way.

Try never.

"Thanks for the picture," she said. "One more to add to my growing collection."

"No problem. You made it seem as if you and Porky travel a lot."

"We do."

"That could be good or bad, depending on your perspective. Where are you two headed this time?"

Finn was hesitant to reveal details of her personal life to anyone, let alone a stranger, but something about Luisa made her want to reveal herself inside and out. There was a word for it in Hungarian. A word that didn't have an English translation. *Szimpatikus*. When you met someone for the first time and your gut told you they were a good person. Finn's instincts told her Luisa was worthy of trust. And a whole lot more.

"Cancún," she said. "What about you?"

"Mexico City."

"The first time I traveled there, the altitude gave me a nosebleed."

Despite the ominous beginning, the trip had turned out to be a pleasant one. Finn had always longed to go back but hadn't been able to find the time. But if Luisa would be waiting for her when she arrived, she would definitely try to fit a flight to Mexico City into her busy travel schedule.

"That happens sometimes," Luisa said, "but the body learns to adjust. Are you headed to Mexico for business or pleasure?"

"A bit of both, actually." Luisa arched her eyebrows in a silent request for more information so Finn tried to fill in some of the blanks without making a fool out of herself in the process. "I'm a writer for *Bon Voyage*, a travel magazine based out of San Francisco, where I live. The editors give contributors twenty-four hours' notice before sending them on a seven-day, all-expenses-paid trip to their next destination."

"And your current assignment is Cancún?"

Finn took another sip of her beer to calm the familiar stirrings of *resfeber*, the Swedish word for the restless beat of a traveler's heart before a journey began.

"Not so much the city itself. That story has been told more times than I can count. There's only so many times you can write about drunk college students puking outside Carlos'n Charlie's or getting into fights in Señor Frog's and make it seem fresh. I've been tasked with writing an article on SOS Tours, a travel agency geared for lesbians. The company's only been in business for about three years and they cater to a niche market, but their footprint is getting bigger every year. They've done cruises until now. Cancún is their first resort trip. Based on the rave reviews they receive from their clientele, it won't be the last. Their first trip was rather inauspicious, though. It was a cruise to the Caribbean, and their first stop on shore was greeted by a horde of anti-gay protesters. After the women poured a shit ton of money into the local economy—I've heard estimates as high as a million dollars—the protests evaporated into pleas for a return visit."

"Money has a way of changing people's minds, if not

their hearts," Luisa said cryptically. Her clouded expression cleared almost as quickly as it had appeared. "Have you done something like this before?"

"Embedding myself with five hundred partying lesbians in various stages of undress, as well as sobriety? No, not even close. My column is called 'Flying Solo.' I focus on what life is like for single travelers, so I'm not used to being part of a group."

And that was just the way she liked it.

In the six years she had been working for *Bon Voyage*, Finn had visited all seven continents at least once, and had more passport stamps than she could count. Not bad for someone who an amateur fortune-teller had once predicted wouldn't travel much.

But her current assignment was the first of its kind. On her previous outings, she had explored her destination on her own, organically and with no predetermined agenda in mind. The perfect gig for someone who preferred being left to her own devices instead of forced to travel in a pack. This time was different. This time, she wasn't being asked to unearth some previously unknown factoid about a selected city but to write a review on one of the fastest-growing companies in the travel business. She was pleased to see a lesbian-owned business thriving in troubled economic times, but she wasn't planning on giving the company a gushing review just because she and the owners shared similar interests. If the women at SOS Tours wanted positive publicity, they would have to earn it.

Luisa's full lips puckered in appreciation. "Your job sounds like fun."

"Except for the occasional travel nightmares, it usually is." Finn felt herself begin to relax and open up the way it was only possible to do with a stranger—or a new friend. "I get a thrill each time my cell phone chirps. Because each incoming email could mean the start of a brand-new adventure."

Luisa shifted in her seat and turned toward Finn. "This might sound like a stupid question, but given such short notice, how do you know what to take with you?"

"That's actually a very good question, not a stupid one." Score one for practicality. "I never know when the call might come, so I keep two bags packed at all times. One for cold climates and another for warm. But all I really need when I travel are a camera and my passport."

"Don't forget about Porky." Luisa grinned mischievously. "And a change of underwear might be nice."

Finn nodded in agreement. "I keep two days' worth in my backpack just in case. I learned that the hard way when I went to Sri Lanka last year and my luggage ended up in Singapore. I wound up going commando, which in certain climates is not as much fun as you might think."

"I'll take your word for it." Luisa shook her head at the bartender's invitation to see a menu. "Since you travel so much, you must have a lot of souvenirs."

Finn shrugged. "Not really. I like to travel light. I don't feel the need to collect trinkets. I collect memories instead. Experiences." Things that wouldn't tie her down and make it difficult to embark on a new journey—or impossible to leave the latest behind. Her nomadic career made relationships difficult, to say the least. It was hard for her to form a lasting connection with someone when she didn't know which city she'd be waking up in from one day to the next. "The only thing I try to bring back from a trip is a word deeply ingrained in the culture I've just visited but has no counterpart in English."

Luisa's smooth brow furrowed in confusion. "Such as?"

"In Japan, for example, there's a word for the sunlight that filters through the leaves of trees. In Brazil, there's a word for the act of running your fingers through your lover's hair. In Norway, there's a word for the euphoria you feel as you begin to fall in love."

"Leave it to the Norwegians to try to describe the indescribable." Finn's heart skipped a beat when Luisa focused her beautiful brown eyes squarely on her. "Tell me more."

Finn took a sip of beer to alleviate a sudden case of dry mouth, then paused to clear her throat.

"In Yaghan, a language indigenous to Tierra del Fuego, Chile, there's a word that's hard to pronounce and even harder to spell—*mamihlapinatapai*."

"What does it mean?" Luisa asked eagerly.

Finn met her expectant gaze. "It's the silent acknowledgment and understanding between two people who are wishing or thinking the same thing but are both unwilling to initiate."

Luisa smiled as if to acknowledge the unspoken fact that the word could be applied to them. "I hate when that happens."

Finn lowered her eyes to watch the slow movement of Luisa's tongue as it curled toward her upper lip to capture a stray bead of beer that hung there. Finn was tempted to lean over and have a taste.

"Yeah, me, too."

Finn tore her eyes away from Luisa and the distracting drop of Corona to give herself time to regain her bearings. She felt at odds. She usually felt like she was walking on air before a trip. Being with Luisa made her feel grounded. She didn't know which surprised her more—that she could feel that way about someone she had just met or that she liked it.

"And on the other end of the spectrum," she said, "there's *ya'aburnee*, an Arabic word that means 'you bury me.' It's a declaration of your desire to die before someone else because it would be too difficult to live without them."

"That describes my parents perfectly. They're like two halves of a whole. They would be lost without each other. Have you ever loved someone that much, Finn?"

Finn didn't have the heart to tell Luisa she had never been in love and didn't have the time or inclination to start now. There were still too many countries she hadn't seen. Too many stories she hadn't written. Too many adventures yet to be taken.

"No. Have you?"

"Not yet."

Finn heard the hopefulness in Luisa's tone and tried to ignore its effect on her. Her relationships, partly by necessity and mostly by design, had always been fleeting. Luisa made her long for something more enduring. Something that lasted longer than a week-long fling in an exotic locale. But that wasn't going to happen. No matter how enticing the bait dangling in front of her—or, in this case, sitting right next to her.

"Tell me about you, Luisa. What do you do?" She hoped the answer would be something boring so she could talk herself into losing interest, but Luisa's response made Finn find her even more intriguing.

"On Monday morning, I officially become a member of the Federal Police."

"You're a *Federale*?" Finn took a longer look at her. She still felt the same sense of authority coming from Luisa, but now it was paired with an air of command. "I can see it now, but on first glance, I would have sworn you were military."

"I used to be. I was in the army for five years before I got tired of my commanding officer's corruption and opted out after my superiors refused to discipline him despite the mountain of evidence I provided to show he was dirty. I was told I should either learn to look the other way or put myself on the narcos' payroll, too. I wasn't willing to accept either solution. From what I hear, I may be in for more of the same when I report for duty on Monday since some of my fellow officers are known for taking bribes, too. I may not succeed, but I hope to change that mentality as soon as I can. If we don't make a stand, the narcos will grow too powerful to be stopped. If we haven't already given them too much of a head start."

Finn could easily picture her as a crusading white knight, but she hoped Luisa wouldn't end up falling on her sword. She wondered how Luisa's predominantly male coworkers would respond to having a woman join their ranks. A woman who was determined to eliminate the under-the-table deals that provided them with much-needed extra income to boot.

"Why did you decide to become a cop?" she asked.

"Because of what my mother likes to call my over-developed sense of honor. I've never been able to turn a blind eye when I see someone doing something illegal or immoral. I feel compelled to do something about it. It seemed only natural for me to decide to do it for a living."

"Even if it means putting your own life at risk?"

Finn had never been able to understand the mentality of soldiers or police officers. They routinely put other people's needs ahead of their own, knowing full well they would receive nothing in return except for marginal support and healthy doses of both contempt and mistrust. How could anyone be that selfless? Did it come naturally or did it develop over time?

"The risk is part of the job," Luisa said with a shrug. "I can't separate one from the other. Nor would I want to. Why do you do what you do?"

"Because it's the only thing I'm good at." The real reason Finn had become a writer was something that went far deeper than her flippant response, but she didn't make a habit out of sharing deep, dark secrets with random strangers. Not even a stranger with a killer smile, beautiful eyes, and a smoking hot body. And Luisa definitely had all three. She raised her beer bottle in a toast. "Good luck with the new gig."

"Thanks. I'll need it." Another dimpled grin. One more and Finn might be tempted to drop trou right there in the bar instead of finding a more discreet location. "Good luck to you, too. With the article, I mean." Luisa drained the rest of her beer, set the empty bottle on the counter, and waved off the bartender's offer of another round. "If you go on vacation for a living," she said, turning back to Finn, "what do you do for fun?"

"I chat up strange women in airport bars."

That answer, unfortunately, was closer to the truth than Finn was willing to admit. She didn't consider herself a pick-up artist by any means, but she preferred fleeting encounters with mutually satisfying conclusions to frustrating delusions of happily ever after.

Luisa rested her elbows on the bar, and her rich alto dropped into an even lower register. Her expression was less come-hither and more come-get-me. "Then this must be my lucky day. Are you a member of the Mile High Club? You must be with so many flights under your belt."

Was she kidding or was she serious? Finn hoped Luisa could tell the difference because she had lost track somewhere between "Is this seat taken?" and "My name's Luisa. What's yours?"

Finn smiled at the memory of a certain flight attendant who had spent most of a sixteen-hour flight to Australia catering to her every need.

"I'll take that as a yes," Luisa said. "Will this be a working vacation for you, or do you plan to have some fun this week?"

Finn tried to determine if they had time to take a taxi to a nearby hotel, check into a room, and put it to use before their respective flights took off. The answer—if she wanted to make it through the long lines at security and back to her gate before it was too late to board her flight—was probably no. But the prospect of spending even a few minutes getting naked with a woman like this was worth the risk.

"I'm game," she said. "What do you have in mind?"

Luisa tossed a twenty-dollar bill on the bar and held out her hand. "Come with me and find out."

❖

Luisa Moreno didn't do things like this. She was the good girl. She played things safe in her personal life. She took risks on the job, but never at home. And she definitely didn't pick up strange women in airport bars. Or anywhere else, for that matter. She preferred relationships, not flings. One-night stands weren't her style. But there was something about Finn Chamberlain that inspired her to do something completely out of her comfort zone. Her head told her coming here was a cautionary tale waiting to happen, but instinct said this was an opportunity not to be missed. When in doubt, she had learned long ago, always go with your gut.

She waved the key card in front of the hotel room door and waited for the light on the electronic sensor to turn green. When she heard the lock click open, she felt something inside her spring free as well.

"After you." She held the door open, and Finn stepped inside. Luisa left her inhibitions in the hall as she followed the gorgeous *gringa* into the room.

The room was nondescript—nothing Luisa hadn't seen before—but Finn was anything but. She was a study in contradictions. Shy, but with the guts of a daredevil. Tall and thin with the body of a jock, but the mind of an intellectual. Her chunky black glasses and ironically humorous T-shirt said nerd, but her fashionably messy brown hair and designer tennis shoes said fashionista. Luisa didn't know which incarnation was the real Finn, but it didn't matter. She was hooked the instant she looked into those piercing blue eyes. She tossed her bag in a corner and turned to face her.

"I don't—" she began, but Finn cut her off with a kiss.

"I know." Finn's hands rested lightly on Luisa's waist, then gently began to rub her sides. Luisa could feel the heat even through the thick cotton of her shirt. "But I do."

Luisa placed her hands on Finn's chest and slowly slid them down until the heels rested on the rise of Finn's breasts. "So what happens next?"

"You assume the position," Finn said with a mischievous smile. "Officer."

Finn twirled a long, tapered finger in the air, indicating she wanted Luisa to turn and face the wall. Luisa complied. Not with the reluctance of a perp, but the eagerness of a lover. She placed her palms on the peeling wallpaper, spread her legs, and waited for the next round in an increasingly sexy game.

Finn began at her feet, her hands gripping her ankles and sliding up her calves. Luisa gasped when Finn's searching hands reached her inner thighs.

"Are you carrying any concealed weapons, Officer? Anything that might stick me or cause me grievous bodily injury?"

Luisa shook her head as Finn cupped her ass. "I plead the Fifth."

Luisa felt Finn's breasts press against her back. Then she felt Finn's breath in her ear, as warm and intoxicating as a shot of well-aged tequila. "You're not allowed to do that."

"Says who?"

"I do." When Luisa turned her head, Finn reached around and gently kneaded her breasts, then captured her lips in a kiss.

Luisa moaned when Finn slid her tongue into her mouth. Teasing. Touching. Exploring. She enjoyed the power play. Giving up her own in order to submit to Finn's. So different from what she was used to. Different and incredibly exciting.

"Am I under arrest?" she asked after Finn finally allowed her to turn and face her again.

"Not yet, but I will have to subject you to a much more thorough search before I decide whether to charge you with something."

"Here. Let me help you." Luisa kicked off her boots, then unzipped her jeans and shimmied out of them. Her underwear quickly followed. When she reached for her Henley, Finn held up a hand to stop her.

"Please allow me."

Luisa released the hem of her shirt and raised her arms over her head. "Since you said please."

Finn peeled off Luisa's shirt, then grazed her knuckles across her belly. Luisa involuntarily flexed her abs in response to the unexpected sensation. Finn's mouth quirked into a smile. "You like that?"

Luisa put her hand on the back of Finn's neck and pulled her closer. "Don't ask questions if you already know the answer."

Finn's smile grew. "I only ask questions if I know the answer's yes."

Luisa pushed Finn on the bed and straddled her body. "Then you must hear 'yes' a lot."

Finn ran her hands up the backs of Luisa's legs. "Upon occasion."

Luisa unbuckled Finn's belt and pulled off her jeans and

thong underwear. Then she reached for Finn's T-shirt, which proclaimed she was once addicted to the hokey pokey but had managed to turn herself around. "We don't have much time," she said, tossing Finn's T-shirt aside and lowering her weight onto Finn's body, "so I might forget to be gentle."

Finn arched her back to meet her. "I was hoping you'd say that."

Luisa glanced at the clock on the nightstand to check the time, then turned the display away from her so she could focus on what really counted: the woman writhing in anticipation beneath her.

Her friends called her "the nun" because she hadn't had sex in so long she had practically become a virgin again. What would her friends say if they could see her now? Probably the same thing her family had said when she'd told them she had decided to join the Federal Police: "What, are you crazy, Luisita?"

If this was what it felt like to be crazy, she decided as Finn's mouth closed around her nipple, she needed to lose her sanity more often. "Tell me what you like."

Finn looked up at her. Luisa had heard that your eyes were the windows to your soul. If that was truly the case, Finn's eyes revealed she was open to adventure. Of all kinds. "I'm flexible."

Luisa placed Finn's knees over her shoulders as she settled between her legs. "I can tell."

She slowly parted Finn's lips with her tongue, savoring the taste of the evidence of Finn's arousal. Finn groaned deep in her throat. Then she gasped when Luisa flicked her tongue against her clit. Once. Twice. On the third stroke, Finn snaked her fingers into Luisa's hair. "That's what I like," she whispered.

Luisa smiled despite herself. Compliments were good to

receive no matter what the setting, but especially one like this. She reached up and pinched one of Finn's nipples between her thumb and forefinger. In response, Finn's guttural moans changed to a high-pitched cry. Luisa wanted more. She wanted to know what Finn sounded like—what she looked like—when she came. She wanted to know what Finn liked for breakfast in the morning and the last thought that crossed her mind before she drifted off to sleep at night.

Even though neither of them had said the words, Luisa knew this was supposed to be a one-time thing, not the start of a relationship. But when Finn came in her mouth—came screaming her name—Luisa knew one time with her would never be enough.

❖

Luisa's mouth was so addictive Finn could have come from the first kiss. Fortunately, Luisa paid as much attention to the rest of her body as she did to her lips. Finn lost count after the third orgasm, but her internal clock told her she needed to get her ass out of bed and back to the airport or she'd miss her flight. But she couldn't leave. Not until she took care of some unfinished business first.

She rolled Luisa onto her back and kissed her way down her body, wondering all the while when she had ever taken a journey she had enjoyed nearly as much. Luisa's body was taut and firm, her smooth skin warm beneath Finn's lips despite the frigid air blasting from the rattling vent strategically placed over the bed.

"We're running out of time," Luisa said.

"I know." Finn chose to ignore rather than heed the warning. "But I need to feel you first." She slid her hand between their bodies, glided through Luisa's wetness, and slipped two fingers inside her. "Are you still ready to leave?" she asked as Luisa began to move against her.

"There you go again." Luisa's voice was husky with desire. "Asking me a question you already know the answer to." She pulled Finn into a kiss that left her breathless from its unexpected combination of tenderness and intensity. A kiss that seemed to embody its initiator. "I don't want you to leave, Finn. I want you to fuck me."

Eager to fulfill Luisa's request, Finn pumped her hand harder. Then she rubbed her thumb against Luisa's clit. She felt Luisa's walls close around her, clenching her fingers and drawing them deeper inside. Luisa sighed in satisfaction. In release. Finn kissed her, wishing they had time to do it all over again.

She didn't know what she had expected when she had agreed to come here, but she definitely hadn't expected this. This sense of connection. Of coming together. Of something that was meant to be.

Being with Luisa was like finding something she didn't know she had been looking for. Something she didn't know she needed. And it was about to end. She wasn't sure she should feel happy that it had happened or sad that it would most likely never happen again.

"Would you like to share the shower to save time?" she asked as she reluctantly rolled out of bed.

Luisa folded her arms behind her head. "I'd love to share many things with you, *mamasita*, but unless you want to show up for your assignment a day late, you'd better not let me anywhere near you when you're wet and naked. Or fully clothed, for that matter. I'll wait my turn and enjoy the show."

Finn paused. "Is this the part where I ask you if we're going to see each other again?"

Luisa's smile was warm and inviting. With no hint

of the brush-off Finn had expected to take place as soon as the afterglow from their final orgasms had faded. The fond farewell she preferred to give rather than receive.

"This is the part where we agree today was something special that probably won't be repeated, but I program my number into your phone when your back is turned in the hope you might find a reason to use it one day."

Finn grinned. "I think I like that part." She impetuously dug her Porky Pig toy out of her backpack and tossed it to Luisa. "Take it. It's yours."

"You're giving me this?" Luisa asked, turning the toy over in her hands.

"A little something for you to remember me by."

Luisa looked skeptical. "Are you sure?"

Finn had owned the toy for nearly twelve years. Porky was never far from her side, whether she was on the road or sitting with her feet up in her apartment. It was hard for her to part with him, but she liked the idea of leaving him with Luisa. And, perhaps, meeting up with the two of them again.

"Maybe, if we're lucky, I'll get a chance to visit him someday."

"Maybe."

Luisa closed her fingers around Porky as if keeping him safe. In that moment, Finn knew she had left him in the right hands. She padded naked to the bathroom, conscious of Luisa's hungry eyes tracking her every movement. She caught herself humming as she allowed the shower's warm spray to wash over her.

She had balked at taking this assignment since it was like nothing she had ever done before. But if every day of the upcoming trip turned out like this one, agreeing to take it might be the best decision she had ever made.

Unless, of course, it didn't.

Despite today's pleasant diversion, she had a bad feeling about this trip. An unexpected sense of dread deep down in her gut. Her instincts had never failed her before, but she hoped against hope now was the first time.

Because if it wasn't, this trip could end up being her last.

Day One

After her plane taxied to a stop and the interminable wait for the doors to open finally ended, Finn hooked her backpack over her shoulder, pulled her carry-on from the overhead bin, and shuffled down the narrow aisle with the tanned golf nuts, lovestruck honeymooners, and fanny pack–wearing seniors with whom she had shared the flight from DFW.

The heat of the tropics never failed to take her by surprise. No matter how many times she tried to prepare herself, her first inhalation of the warm, humid air was like breathing underwater. She slipped her sunglasses on as she descended the airplane's steps and walked across the tarmac toward the small but bustling airport.

"Here we go."

She strolled past the anxious passengers waiting for their luggage to appear in the baggage claim area and joined the long line at Customs, wondering if she would be blessed with a bored agent who barely looked at her or an overly officious one who asked a million questions and stared at her passport photo as if committing it to memory before finally waving her through the line. The agent she received was thankfully somewhere in between. Polite, efficient, and absolutely adorable.

"Man," Finn said under her breath as she tucked her passport away and headed for the exit, "I am such a sucker for a woman in uniform."

Even, it turned out, if the woman was out of uniform at the time. She smiled as she remembered the ninety minutes of athletic sex she had shared with Luisa Moreno that afternoon. Traveling through Dallas in the future would never be the same.

Finn followed the sign pointing the way to ground transportation. She wouldn't have to worry about hailing a cab and haggling over the fare, however. According to the reams of documentation she had received from Brett, SOS Tours provided free transfers to and from the airport for its guests. She moved past brightly dressed men and women holding up signs emblazoned with the names of various hotels, resorts, and tour groups and focused on a pert blonde in a pastel polo shirt and white cargo shorts. The placard in her hand read, "SOS."

"Looking for me?" the blonde asked with a friendly and slightly flirtatious smile.

"Yes, I believe I am."

"Welcome to Sisters of Sappho." The blonde stuck out her hand. "I'm Katie Walker. I'll be working with the Indies this week."

"The what?"

"Indies are what we at SOS call our independent travelers." Katie lowered her voice to a conspiratorial whisper. "'Indie' holds less stigma than 'single' and it's much more encompassing. Being an Indie doesn't necessarily mean you're not in a relationship. It simply means you're traveling alone. Are you an Indie?"

"In every sense of the word."

"Great." Katie reached into the messenger bag slung

across her shoulder and pulled out a ball and chain necklace containing a dog tag branded with the SOS Tours logo. "Wear this to help you locate your fellow Indies and to help them find you. We have all sorts of fun activities planned for you this week, including a beach barbecue, a sunset cruise, and several excursions into town, so I promise you won't have time to get bored or lonely. The bus is located in spot number twenty-nine. Sasha will check your name off the master list and get you on your way. Have fun. I'll see you back at the resort."

"Thanks."

Finn felt like she had just strolled into a perky buzz saw. She walked down the row of idling charter buses and passenger vans until she reached the bus parked in the space numbered twenty-nine, where dozens of women—coupled, alone, or in groups—crowded around a sporty-looking redhead wielding a name-filled clipboard. The redhead's name tag said her name was Sasha Greene. She looked like a cross between a personal trainer and a drill sergeant. Finn wasn't surprised to see she was SOS Tours' activities director.

Sasha ticked off the names of a pair of silver-haired women in matching tie-dye T-shirts, affixed their last names and room numbers to their luggage, and watched as the bags were loaded into the bus's storage area. When they arrived at the hotel, resort employees would take the guests' bags from the bus to their rooms so the guests wouldn't have to lug them all over kingdom come, but Finn was too anal to let her bags out of her sight. She had lost too much luggage over the years to trust it to someone else, no matter how well meaning.

"Next," Sasha said to a group of dog tag–wearing Indies traveling in a pack.

"I have regrets older than they are."

Finn turned to find an African American woman in a spiked bra top, leather hot pants, and six-inch stiletto heels.

Finn didn't know which was the more badass accessory, the woman's hot pink Mohawk or her Harley-inspired motorized wheelchair. The woman's name was even more dramatic than her appearance.

"Aurora Bennett. Is this your first SOS trip?"

"Yes, yours?"

Aurora unleashed a brassy laugh. "Not hardly. This is my tenth. I wouldn't travel any other way."

Finn had heard there were women who didn't plan a vacation unless SOS or its main business rival, Olivia Travel, was involved, but she had never been able to understand the allure of paying someone to do something she could do herself. And for far less money. Who needed an expensive travel agent or a costly tour company when the Internet was free?

"What makes you keep coming back to SOS?" she asked.

"The trips are pricy. I'm not going to lie about that. But having the chance to be completely myself without being judged and to surround myself in the company of women is priceless. Give it a few days. You'll see what I mean."

After she checked in with Sasha and found a seat on the rapidly filling bus, Finn pulled her notebook out of her backpack and began jotting down her first impressions of SOS Tours and its colorful array of clients.

"'Dear Diary,'" Aurora said teasingly as Sasha carried her down the aisle and deposited her into the seat next to Finn. "'I met a beautiful ebony goddess today and I think I'm in love.' Does that sound about right?"

"Close, but no cigar."

"Then what are you writing?"

Finn hesitated. Not wanting their dining experiences to be tainted by discovery of why they were there, food critics ate in anonymity and wrote their reviews in private. She had planned to do the same. But instead of blending in with the crowd, she was standing out from it. Just like old times.

She put her notebook away and took advantage of the opportunity to have a conversation with someone other than the barista at her favorite coffeehouse or the owner of the small independent bookstore where she researched her upcoming destination before each trip.

"Why write when I can talk to the beautiful ebony goddess who has stolen my heart?"

Aurora chucked Finn under her chin. "You're cute, but I have regrets older than you, too."

"How old are you?"

Aurora belted herself into her seat. "Old enough to know better than to answer that question. Why don't you ask what's really on your mind? It's the first thing most people want to know."

Finn thought of the wheelchair now residing in the bus's oversized storage compartment, but curiosity led her in a different direction. "How did you get your unique sense of style?"

Aurora laughed again. "Oh, you are a charmer. If I were an indeterminate number of years younger, I would be on you like white on rice. Give me enough champagne cocktails and I still might be. Are you spoken for?"

"I'm an Indie." Finn indicated the colorful dog tag around her neck.

Aurora rolled her eyes. "Girl, you *are* new at this. Not all Indies are single. Some are simply halves of adventurous couples looking to add spice to their relationships. I know of at least three on this bus alone who would give you good money to rent that necklace from you for a night or two."

Finn looked around the bus. Her fellow passengers

seemed too straitlaced to fit Aurora's description, but perhaps they were too tired from their respective flights to let their hair down so soon. "So these trips are pretty much anything goes?"

"They can be, but I've never known any of the women to be as bad as the boys. An all-gay tour group rented the resort last week. I heard from some people in the know that a few of the guests offered the security guards twenty bucks each for a blow job. More than half of hotel employees down here make an average of five bucks a day, so the line to dish out BJs was longer than you might think."

"Does that surprise you?"

"Nothing surprises me. When the drinks are all-inclusive, people's true natures come out—or at least the ones they don't want anyone at home to see."

Finn thought about the reckless move she had made going to a hotel with Luisa Moreno after one beer and twenty minutes of conversation. Had that been her true nature or a mistake she still might live to regret?

Sasha stood at the front of the bus and raised her hands to get everyone's attention. "Welcome to Cancún," she said into a handheld radio hooked into the bus's PA system. "Who's ready to party?"

The answering roar was so loud Finn thought she might have accidentally wandered into a 49ers game.

"Emilio, our trusty bus driver, will take you to our home for the week, the Mariposa Resort and Spa. My SOS teammates are waiting to greet you. After you arrive, they'll escort you to the theater. While you enjoy a refreshing beverage, my teammates and the resort staff will take your passports, match them up with your reservations, then return them to you, along with your room keys. After you check in, the afternoon will be yours to enjoy. Explore the resort, take a walk on the beach, introduce yourself to old friends, or make some new ones. Whatever you decide to do, don't forget to return to the theater in time for tonight's show. We have a wonderful lineup of performers eager to entertain you this week, and we'll kick it off tonight with Rusty Connors."

SOS certainly didn't scrimp when it came to providing quality entertainment for its guests, Finn thought. Rusty Connors was one of the leading lights on the lesbian comedy circuit. Four more comediennes were scheduled to take the stage at some point over the next seven nights, along with a spoken-word artist and a musician who had finished a close second on one of those singing competitions American television networks broadcast ad nauseam.

After Sasha hopped off the bus to wait for the next wave of arrivals, Emilio closed the doors and began the short drive from the airport to the hotel. The ride was hairy but not as frightening as some Finn had experienced in the past. On her first trip to Acapulco, for example, she had lost count of the number of times her life had flashed before her eyes as the driver sped around the hairpin curves, displaying way too much confidence in the flimsy guardrail that prevented him and his passengers from taking a nasty drop to the rocks five thousand feet below.

When the bus pulled up at the Mariposa Resort and Spa, twenty smiling SOS Tours employees and a smattering of the resort's large staff, all dressed in color-coordinated polo shirts, were standing out front. They clapped rhythmically, keeping time with the SOS Tours theme song blasting from the in-ground speakers lining the cobblestone driveway.

Finn heard effusive cries of greeting as the passengers began to disembark. Aurora was welcomed like a conquering hero. When it was her turn to walk through the two-sided receiving line, Finn expected the smiles she received to be plastic and forced, but they actually seemed genuine.

"No wonder so many travelers are addicted to this."

A resort staffer reached for her carry-on. "Would you like me to take your bags to your room?"

"No, thanks. I can take care of it myself."

There were three hundred rooms spread around the expansive grounds, and she didn't want to risk having her luggage end up parked outside the wrong one. If that happened, it could be hours or even days before they were reunited. The minor headache of lugging them around now prevented the major headache of potentially losing track of them later.

Finn followed the crowd to the air-conditioned theater and took a seat near the back of the room while the laborious—and occasionally riotous—check-in process began.

"What do you mean my room isn't ready?" a woman in several layers of cold-weather gear asked when her passport was returned minus the promised room key. "My wife and I have taken three planes and a bus to get here. We've been traveling for hours. We could use a shower and a change of clothes."

"I understand your frustration," a harried SOS employee said, "but the resort was completely full last week and it will be next week as well. The staff needs time to conduct the changeover. They're working as fast as they can. Please have a little patience."

"But—"

"We're on vacation, Jules," her partner said. "Let's have a beer in the bar and wait for our friends. We can sort everything else out later."

Jules started to protest further but changed her mind. "Sounds like a plan to me."

"Crisis averted." The staffer—her name tag read Verity—heaved an exaggerated sigh. She took Finn's passport with a chirpy, "Be right back. Would you like something to drink in the meantime?"

Finn fanned herself with the hem of her T-shirt. "A cold beer would be great."

"Light or dark?"

Finn took note of the plastic mugs of beer being delivered all around the room and opted for the ale over the lager. "Light's fine."

"Awesome. I'll have one sent over to you. This is your first trip with SOS, isn't it? Do you have any questions?"

"As a matter of fact, I do. Is being cheerful all the time a prerequisite to becoming a member of the staff?"

Verity grinned. "No, but it certainly helps. I'll be back in a flash."

Finn's beer arrived in a matter of minutes, but her passport was returned before she had made it halfway through her drink. She expected to hear another version of the "have a little patience" routine, but Verity smiled and said, "Your room's ready." She held up a clear plastic wristband branded with the resort's name and a flock of butterflies. "Left or right?"

Finn held out her right arm. "What's this for?" she asked as Verity fastened the band around her wrist.

"The beaches in Mexico are public, so guests from the other hotels often wander onto the other properties. The wristbands allow the hotel owners to tell which guests belong where. The edges are deceptively sharp, though, so be careful when you take a shower or you could accidentally slice off a nipple."

"Nice."

"If you'll follow me, I'll show you to your room."

Finn polished off the rest of her beer, then followed Verity on a brief tour of the resort, walking past three bars, four buffet-style restaurants, a gift shop, a fitness center, an infirmary, the on-site office of the external tour group in charge of optional excursions, and a media room featuring computers that offered high-speed Internet access for a nominal fee. She planned to hit all the bars and restaurants, burn off some high-calorie meals in the fitness center, and pay a visit to the excursion office during her stay, but the media room didn't rank high on her list of priorities. If she wanted to check the goings-on in the outside world, she could use the WiFi on her smartphone. *Thank God for international service plans.* Otherwise, the surcharge for the data she used during her frequent forays out of the country would be astronomical.

She paused when a speedboat came roaring into the lagoon. The driver, a shirtless hotel employee with skin burnished bronze by prolonged exposure to the sun, waited until the last possible moment to cut the speed and allow the boat to drift to the tie-off spot next to a rock wall separating the lagoon from the Olympic-size pool. Then he hopped out of the boat and took another one out for a spin.

"The speedboats are available for rent, if you like," Verity said. "You can get behind the wheel, go out in groups of two or four, drive out to a private island a few miles away, and have a picnic. Only one hundred fifty dollars for two hours. The more people you have, the less you pay."

"Not my cup of tea," Finn said as they started walking again. Her favorite adventures involved muscle power, not horsepower, which was why the zip-lining excursion and the half-day walking tour of Chichén Itzá she had seen advertised in the window of the external tour group's office had captured her attention. She might have to add one or both to her still-forming agenda.

"Here we are." Verity stopped in front of a sky blue brick building labeled, appropriately enough, Azul. "Your room's on the third floor. There's no elevator, but there's a set of stairs on each end of the building. Would you like me to take one of your bags?"

"If you insist."

This close to her final destination, Finn finally felt comfortable handing over her carry-on. Verity gave it an experimental heft and seemed surprised by its light weight.

"You didn't pack much. I hope you plan to participate in the theme nights. Disco Night's new, but the White Party is a crowd favorite."

"I'm more of an observer than a joiner."

Verity tossed a wink over her shoulder as she climbed the stairs. "I'll see what I can do to change that. Your room is down here on the corner. Everyone gets free turndown service in the afternoon. So if you leave your room to explore the resort and pop back in just before dinner, don't be surprised to find chocolates on your pillow and a bath towel shaped like the animal of the day on the foot of your bed. The peacocks are a real crowd favorite."

Verity unlocked the door and ushered Finn inside. A queen-sized bed, a stocked mini-bar, a closet, a full bathroom, and a small seating area were squeezed into less than four hundred square feet. The room's relatively small space was more than offset by the spectacular views.

"From the balcony, you can see the lagoon on one side and the beach on the other."

Finn joined Verity on the balcony and looked back at the lagoon, where brightly colored tropical birds perched in the trees and a stingray went for a lazy late-afternoon swim.

"There used to be a crocodile living in the lagoon, but he got too big and scared the guests so the resort had to move him to a new home," Verity said.

Finn turned from the dark brown water of the lagoon to

the crystal-clear waters of the Caribbean Sea. "Um, why are there armed guards on the beach?"

The resort's cadre of security guards wore pristine white uniforms. The gunmen riding ATVs on the beach were dressed in army-issue camouflage and carried AK-47s instead of walkie-talkies.

Verity let out a nervous laugh. "They're here to protect us. As you may know, Mexico is home to several drug cartels. One of the most powerful, the Jaguars, calls Cancún home."

"Should I be concerned for my safety?"

"Of course not. It's perfectly safe. If it wasn't, the owners and management of SOS Tours would never have decided to put its brand on the line by coming here. There are dozens of hotel properties lining the beach and I can honestly say there's never been an incident."

Finn looked at the string of multimillion-dollar hotels that stretched as far as the eye could see and the hundreds, if not thousands of tourists cavorting in the sun, seemingly without care.

"That's comforting."

"The guards patrol the beach around the clock," Verity said. "They may move from one end to the other from time to time to check things out, but they're always around just in case."

Finn felt the butterflies in her stomach flap their wings a little harder. "It's the 'just in case' that worries me."

❖

Luisa cranked up the air conditioner and stripped down to her tank top after she finished lugging the last of six oversized boxes up the four flights of stairs to her apartment overlooking Republic Square, the home of the Monument to the Revolution. Her heart pounded in her chest and her head swam as she struggled to readjust to the thin air of her nation's capital.

"I've been out of the country too long."

She had been staying with her parents since she got out of the army. Texas was much too flat to compete with Mexico City's altitude.

"I should have organized a moving party," she said breathlessly as she surveyed the hours of work that needed to be done before she could pronounce her new surroundings livable. Except her family lived in Dallas now, and her friends were split between Juárez, where she had grown up, and Guadalajara, where she used to serve. For the first time in her life, she was on her own. "Looks like I have to get used to my own company for a while."

The thought of spending the coming days and, possibly, weeks alone made her think of Finn traveling the world by herself and detailing her adventures for readers eager to live vicariously through her.

Luisa located the Porky Pig figurine Finn had given her in Dallas and set it on the coffee table. Seeing the toy reminded her of Finn and the brief time they had spent together that afternoon. It also made her long for more. Was Finn enjoying her latest outing, she wondered, or was she itching for something more exciting than free drinks and poolside party games?

Luisa was tempted to call her, but reaching out this soon could be considered a sign of desperation, loneliness, or both. So far, only one of those adjectives applied. She didn't want to go for two. So she busied herself putting her apartment in order and hoped her life would follow suit.

She wasn't used to being without a support system. She always had her parents, extended family, or friends around to talk her through a crisis or to celebrate her latest achievement. But things were different now. Now she had enemies on both sides of the law gunning for her. All because she had dared to try to change the status quo.

Drug kingpins, commonly referred to as narcos in Mexico, routinely paid off local, state, and federal officials, as well as journalists and ordinary citizens, to curry favor or facilitate their efforts to conduct their illegal trade. Some recipients of the bribes weren't given a choice as to whether to take the substantial sums they were offered. Their lives, as well as the lives of their friends and family members, were threatened if they tried to hold out.

Luisa's commanding officer, however, had been all too willing to receive the weekly payoffs. He had taken the envelopes with a smile on his face and purchased all sorts of expensive toys with his ill-gotten gains. A fancy car, an expensive house, and a luxurious watch, for starters. Three things he wouldn't have been able to afford if he wasn't on the take.

When she had reported what she knew, her CO had painted a much different picture for the investigators following up on her claims. He had admitted receiving the bribes, but he had lowballed the amount and said he had only accepted the money in order to protect his wife and children from harm. He had offered to pay restitution by making a donation to charity for the same amount he had received. The few thousand pesos he had given to a local orphanage probably didn't amount to one week's payout, let alone a year's worth of cash-filled envelopes.

Somehow, though, he had survived the scandal unscathed and Luisa's reputation was the one that had wound up tarnished. Some of her colleagues called her a turncoat to her face. Others called her a rat behind her back.

"You would have done the same thing if the narcos had come to you," they said. "Maybe you already have and you're trying to get a bigger piece of the pie."

The only thing she had ended up with was a target on her back. And no matter how much she hated being alone, she couldn't afford to let anyone get too close or they might get caught in the crossfire. It was hard enough putting herself at risk day in and day out. She didn't want to endanger the lives of anyone she loved in the process.

When all her belongings were put away and the boxes were broken down and discarded down the trash chute, she rewarded herself with the bag of tacos she had purchased from a street vendor on the corner. *Lengua* tacos and *tacos al pastor*, a flavorful combination of onions, cilantro, pineapples, salsa, and thinly sliced pork that could be found anywhere Mexican food was sold but never tasted as good as it did in the capital. Eating *tacos al pastor* was like coming home, though she felt a pang of guilt when she spied the Porky Pig figurine standing sentry on the coffee table.

"Sorry about the meal, Porky. Don't look too close, okay?"

She nuked the tacos in the microwave for a couple of minutes, then settled in front of the TV to watch her favorite soccer team try to break its three-game losing streak. Her cell phone rang after she finished her first taco and was reaching for a second. On the TV screen, the striker for Las Chivas was preparing to take a shot at the opposing goal. Luisa rose from her seat in anticipation and cursed when the shot went wide.

"Keep this up and you'll end up relegated to second division." Disgusted by the easy miss, she brought her phone to her ear without bothering to check the display. "Moreno."

"How's my favorite *Federale*?"

Luisa couldn't place the voice at first. Then she closed her eyes and imagined its owner calling her name. "Finn."

"Sounds like you're at a party. Am I interrupting something?"

"No." Luisa picked up the remote and muted the TV. "I was watching soccer, but my team's losing as usual. What about you? What are you up to?"

"It's seafood night in all the restaurants so I just finished dining on shrimp, lobster, and fresh fish with five hundred of my closest friends."

Luisa glanced at the greasy paper bag sitting on her coffee table. "Your meal puts mine to shame, that's for sure."

"What are you having?"

"*Tacos de lengua.*"

"*Lengua* means 'tongue,' doesn't it? I don't think I could ever eat anything that can taste me, too."

"Are you sure about that? Because you seemed perfectly fine with the concept a few hours ago." So had she. "Are you calling to set up another meeting, are you trying to make me jealous of your five-star meal, or are you simply checking up on how Porky likes his new digs?"

Luisa picked up the small figurine and regarded its well-worn features.

"I'm sure Porky's settling in just fine," Finn said. "The real reason I'm calling is to ask what you know about the Jaguars."

The unexpected seriousness in Finn's tone made Luisa's antennae go up. She put the toy down and gave Finn her full attention. "I assume you mean the Mexican drug cartel, not the American football team."

"I do."

"Why are you asking about them?"

"One of the staffers with SOS let it slip that the Jaguars are very active in the area. I read about the massacres that went on several years ago when dozens of tourists were kidnapped and killed. I want to make sure I don't find myself in the middle of a situation I don't want to be in."

Luisa chose her words carefully before she responded. "I won't tell you there's nothing to fear because that isn't true. The Jaguars are one of the most dangerous cartels in all of Mexico. Their leader is shadowy. The authorities don't know who he is or what he looks like."

"So he could be anyone."

And that was the most frustrating part of trying to catch him. The list of viable suspects was short and most of the names on it had already been discounted. Someone out there wielded tremendous power and influence, but who?

"The identity of the Jaguars' leader is as much a mystery as the group's sudden rise to power," Luisa said. "Los Zetas used to be the largest cartel in the country, but the Jaguars have taken over most of their territory."

"Based on what I'm hearing from you, it sounds like I should catch the next flight out of here."

"No, that's not what I said." Luisa hadn't meant for her candor to frighten Finn into leaving. Powerful—and violent—drug cartels had existed in Mexico for decades. Though their clashes with citizens were commonplace, their run-ins with tourists were a rarity. "You're staying at the Mariposa, correct?"

"Yes," Finn said warily.

"I'm familiar with their security setup. They have guards everywhere and my guys are on the beach. The Jaguars are vicious and they love publicity, but they aren't crazy. Tourists are their customers, too. They aren't going to bite the hand that feeds them. And if they did try to make a move on the Mariposa or any of the hotels along the beach, they wouldn't stand a chance. The patrols and monitoring systems are just too good."

"Thanks, Luisa." The relief in Finn's voice was almost palpable. "I have to go. I'm late for tonight's show. But do you think I could call you tomorrow when we have more time to talk?"

"Do you need me to give you another civics lesson?"

"Maybe I just need to hear your voice. Would that be okay?"

The longing Luisa heard in Finn's voice matched the yearning she felt in her own heart. About to start a new job far away from home, friends, and family, she needed a connection. And, perhaps, she had formed one with Finn Chamberlain. But how could she invite Finn into her world when doing so could put Finn's life at risk?

Finn was safe, she told herself. Hundreds of miles away and protected by armed guards twenty-four hours a day. What harm could come of a few telephone conversations?

"I'd like that," she said before she could change her mind. "What's tomorrow night's meal, caviar and *foie gras*?"

"The theme's Italian, so I imagine not."

"You'll have to tell me all about it while I'm eating beans out of a can."

"I will." Finn's chuckle reminded Luisa yet again of that afternoon in Dallas. Their brief meeting at the bar and their longer encounter in the hotel nearby. She couldn't get either out of her mind. "Good night, Luisa."

"Good night, Finn."

Luisa ended the call with a smile on her face. Her life was as uncertain as ever, but with one phone call, it had suddenly become a lot less lonely.

Day Two

Finn's sides ached from laughing. Rusty Connors had been even funnier in person than she was on the comedy album Finn had downloaded for background research before her trip. Finn ran some of the best bits from last night's show through her head as she walked from her room to the center of the resort. The lounge chairs circling the pool were empty, but blue beach towels marked them as claimed, their owners either strolling on the beach or grazing on the sumptuous breakfast buffet.

Deciding to work on her tan another day, Finn found a shaded cabana and climbed onto the overstuffed cushion. She pulled her electronic reader out of her backpack, but soon found herself doing more people watching than reading.

To her left, artisans began setting up their stalls so anyone with an artistic bent could decorate their own hand-painted souvenirs. To her right, tourists wearing a veritable rainbow of wristbands wandered the beach. The male ones seemed confused by the large number of women on Mariposa's end of the beach. Their facial expressions were almost comical when they seemed to realize the reason why. Some did quick U-turns, others slowed to a crawl so they could get a closer look. Finn stifled a laugh when one lookie-loo did a face plant while ogling a couple making out in the sand. Then a commotion farther up the beach drew her attention away from the embarrassed peeping Tom.

When she saw a lifeguard carrying a limp woman in his arms, she thought someone must have had too much sun or gotten into trouble in the water. Then she noticed the lifeguard was heading toward the water instead of away from it. Her breath caught when she saw Aurora's hot pink Mohawk sticking up over his shoulder.

"Is she—She can't be."

But she was.

The lifeguard placed Aurora on a plastic lounge chair and, with the help of another lifeguard and several SOS staffers, carried the chair over a sand dune. Then they gently transferred Aurora, wearing a leopard print life vest, from the chair to the water.

Aurora floated on the waves with a beatific smile on her face as the lifeguards and staffers made sure her head remained above the water.

Tears welled in Finn's eyes as she watched the tenderness with which Aurora's handlers treated her, and she saw the trust—and peace—in Aurora's expression.

"Would you like something to drink?" a passing waiter asked, pen pad at the ready.

Finn had brought a bottle of water from her room, and it was too early for her to order something stronger. "Nothing for me, thanks." She pointed toward Aurora. "But give that woman a champagne cocktail when she's done. Give her a message for me, too. Tell her Finn said she gets it now."

The waiter looked confused as he recorded both her drink order and her message on his pen pad. "Anything you say, *señorita*."

Finn shook her head in wonder as she wiped her eyes.

"One day in, and I'm already drinking the Kool-Aid."

Being around so many people always put her on edge. She was more comfortable in crowds of five or six, not five hundred. Noise-canceling headphones did the trick during long airplane flights or even longer train rides, but she couldn't wear them all week without appearing rude or standoffish. Last night's comedy show had helped her relax a bit, but talking to Luisa was what had truly put her mind at ease. Why couldn't she meet someone who made her feel like this every day? Or did knowing she and Luisa most likely didn't have a future make it so easy for her to enjoy the present?

She reinvented herself on each trip, becoming the person she needed to be to suit the task at hand. With Luisa, it was different. She didn't need to be someone else. She only needed to be herself. Was that enough for Luisa, or would her interest in Finn end as soon as they began their next respective assignments?

"Speaking of assignments."

Finn pulled out her phone and texted Brett to let her know she had arrived safely.

Better late than never, Brett texted back. *Have you started working the story? If so, what approach have you decided to take? Should I expect to receive a regular column or a straightforward review?*

Finn hadn't made up her mind yet. She had taken copious notes since she had arrived, but she hadn't started trying to figure out how to cobble them into a cohesive story yet.

My narrative changes by the day, she wrote. *I think I'll wait until the end of the week and type up something during my flight back to the States or while I'm sitting in an airport bar during a layover.*

Unless, of course, a hot Mexican woman who worked for the Federal Police plopped on the bar stool next to hers and distracted her from the task at hand. No, that was too much to ask. Something that good could happen only once in a lifetime.

"You look way too serious for someone who's supposed to be on vacation."

Finn looked up to find one of her dinner companions from last night standing in front of her cabana.

Indies had designated tables set aside for them in all the resort's restaurants so they wouldn't have to eat alone. Last night, Finn had been sandwiched between Jill Elliott and Ryan Norris, best friends from Toronto who were making their third SOS trip.

She tried to recall their biographical details. If she remembered correctly, Jill was a paramedic and Ryan was a firefighter. Or was it the other way around? Whatever her profession happened to be, Jill was standing in front of her wearing a black sports bra and a pair of maple leaf-accented board shorts, but Ryan was MIA.

"Where's your partner in crime?" Finn asked as she put her phone in her backpack for safekeeping.

"Chatting up someone she met at the omelet station during breakfast service."

"You don't sound too happy about that," Finn said before remembering Jill had a rather large unrequited crush on her friend and roommate.

Jill shrugged with studied nonchalance. "I'm happy if she's happy. She still comes home to me at the end of the night, so I guess that's the most I can hope for. Do you mind if I invade your space for a few minutes while I wait for the water aerobics to finish?"

In the pool, a buff instructor in a bright orange string bikini was leading about thirty women through moves that looked alternately silly and taxing. The water provided both resistance and a cushion as the women bounced, splashed, and laughed their way through an hour-long workout. The up-tempo dance music blaring from the PA system gradually gave way to more relaxing sounds, alerting onlookers that the strenuous part of the session had ended and the post-workout cooldown had begun.

"Have a seat."

Jill climbed into the cabana and made herself at home on the far end. Her freckled face already bore the telltale pink hue of a budding case of sunburn. Under a plethora of tattoos, the skin of her broad shoulders was the same color as her strawberry blond hair.

"You're a writer, aren't you?" Jill asked, resting her hands on her knees.

During dinner the night before, conversation had inevitably turned from what everyone had selected from the buffet to what they did for a living. Finn had said she was a writer, but she hadn't specified what kind. Big mistake. For the rest of the night, she had been cornered by a slew of women eager to tell her their life stories so she could use the details as fodder for a future book. Too bad she wasn't a romance novelist. If she were, she had enough story ideas to craft at least a dozen books. And today was only the second day.

"How do you do that?" Jill asked. "How do you put your thoughts on paper and have them make sense? I can talk to anyone—the phrase 'never met a stranger' was probably invented for me—but I can't write for shit."

"For me, the opposite is true. Writing has always come easy. It's talking that's hard. On paper, I can be witty, challenging, and thoughtful. In person, I'm a tongue-tied doofus who can't string two words together without stammering and thinks of the best response to a comment five minutes after it's too late to use it."

"Sounds like we could help each other out."

"I can be the Cyrano to your Christian?"

Jill knitted her eyebrows in confusion as she scratched her reddened shoulder. "Who?"

"Never mind," Finn said, deciding that unlimited free drinks and references to classic literature didn't mix.

"Do you want to be on my team during the pool games?"

"What are they, anyway?" Finn remembered seeing a listing for them at noon on the daily schedule, but no description had been provided to give her an idea of what they might entail.

"They could be anything. Sometimes it's a relay race where team members have to pass a water balloon from one end of the line to the other without using their hands. Sometimes you play water polo or paddle kayaks for a lap of the pool. My favorite, though, is Gladiator. In that one, you stand on a surfboard armed with a padded baton that looks like a Q-tip on steroids and try to knock your opponent off her board and into the water."

"Sounds interesting." If a bit painful.

"So is that a yes?" Jill asked hopefully.

Finn weighed the merits of potentially going home with a black eye against the thousands of words of copy the experience might provide.

"Count me in."

"Awesome," Jill said with a broad grin that quickly faded into another frown. "I wish telling Ryan how I feel about her was that easy."

"What have you tried so far?"

"Everything short of a lap dance."

"Specifically."

"She isn't a hearts and flowers kind of girl, as you can probably tell. I took her to a Leafs game last year and told her I loved her at halftime, but she either didn't hear what I said or didn't take me seriously. She ended up going home with some chick she met in the bathroom line."

"I'm sensing a theme here. Note to self: don't stand in a line with Ryan unless you're looking to get picked up."

Jill laughed and crossed her legs at the ankles like she was trying to assume a complicated yoga pose. "See? You can be funny in person, too, not just in print."

"Good to know."

"You're a cool girl," Jill said, eying Finn's Indie necklace. "Why are you single?"

"I'm on the road a lot."

"Researching your books?"

"Something like that. It's not easy to sustain a relationship when you're never home."

"Maybe you'll meet someone here and you could have a vacationship. Isn't that what they call it when two people are dating but they live in different cities and only see each other when they're on vacation?"

"Vacationship." Finn swirled the word around her mouth like she was sampling a glass of wine. "That's a new one for the memory bank. I'll have to work it into a column." She caught her error and quickly corrected it. "I mean novel."

Jill beamed. "Remember you heard it here first. Don't forget to give me a shout-out in the acknowledgments. It might be the only way my name ever winds up in a book."

"You got it."

"Sisters of Sappho," Rusty Connors said into a cordless microphone as she approached the pool, "are you ready to get wet and wild?"

"That's our cue. Let's go." Jill grabbed Finn's hand and pulled her out of the cabana.

"What about my stuff?" Finn pointed to her backpack and beach towel. "Where should I store my things?"

Jill waved her hand dismissively.

"Leave everything where it is. No one's going to touch anything that doesn't belong to them. Everyone respects each other's property on these trips. On my last one, I saw a woman digging through the trash in the bathroom because she'd lost a six-carat diamond ring. She thought she'd never see it again, but someone turned it in to Lost and Found the same day."

Finn felt like she had wandered onto the set of a Frank Capra movie. When she saw the pair of five-woman teams forming in the shallow end of the pool, she knew she was living a wonderful life indeed. The contestants weren't universally young, supermodel thin, or classically beautiful, but they were all comfortable with themselves, at ease with each other, and eager to compete.

"Huddle up, my little dykelings." Rusty's molasses-thick Oklahoma drawl grew even more syrupy the longer she spent baking under the midday sun. "You have five minutes to put your heads together and come up with your team names."

Finn's teammates turned toward her. "You're the writer," one said. "Think of something creative."

Naturally, Finn's mind went blank. "When I was in college, my roommate played on an intramural softball team called the '69ers."

"Who hasn't?" someone said with a snicker.

"If it gets me laid tonight, I'm okay with it," said a woman with considerably more salt than pepper in her close-cropped hair. "There may be snow on the roof, but there's still fire in the furnace, girls. Now let's kick some ass."

Rusty briefly conferred with both teams to gather their team names. "All right, my sisters. Today's game is Gladiator. Or, as I like to call it, Battling Babes on Boards. Today's matchup will feature the '69ers taking on the Fabulous Femmes." She lifted a carefully sculpted eyebrow toward her platinum blond hair. "Sounds like an average Saturday night in my house."

"We got this in the bag," Jill said.

"I don't know." Finn took a long look at the members of the opposing team. "Some of those femmes look like they've been hitting the gym pretty hard."

Two SOS Tours staffers swam to the middle of the pool and demonstrated the game while four resort employees held on to the surfboards to keep them steady. The SOS staffers swatted at each other at half-speed until one took a shot to the midsection and fell into the water with a melodramatic flourish.

"Who wants to go first?" Rusty asked after the demonstration ended.

"You have the most experience, Jill," Finn said. "Why don't you lead off?"

"I said Gladiator was my favorite game. I never said I was any good at it. But I'll try to put us on the board."

Jill and one of the Fabulous Femmes swam to the middle of the pool.

"No blows to the head or face," Rusty said after Jill and her opponent climbed on their respective surfboards and struggled to maintain their balance. "Aside from that, it's anything goes. But remember it's all in fun. Ready, ladies? On three. One. Two. Three."

Both competitors began to swing. Finn flinched as heavy blows thudded against shoulders, arms, and legs. Perhaps the extra words of copy weren't worth the bruises after all. But the competition had already started. It was too late to back out now.

In for a penny, in for a pound.

Jill won her bout in about five seconds flat, but the '69ers lost the next two. By the time it was Finn's turn, the score was tied at four and her match would prove to be the deciding one.

"No pressure," she said under her breath as she tried to find her balance on the surfboard.

"Stay low and spread your feet," she heard Jill say. "Make her come to you."

"Stay low? Make her come?" Rusty fanned herself with a copy of the day's program. "Is it just me or is it getting hot out here? Sorry. I was having a personal moment for a second there. In the final match of the day, we have Finn from the '69ers taking on Amy from the Fabulous Femmes. Let's hear it for them!"

Amy was at least six inches taller than Finn and her arms were so long Finn didn't think she'd be able to penetrate her defenses. Thankfully, though, Amy wasn't much of a strategist. With her girlfriend cheering her on from the sidelines, she went for the win right away. But her wild swing and subsequent miss threw her off balance. When Finn recovered her bearings, she pressed the tip of her padded baton into Amy's ribs and pushed as hard as she could. Amy dropped one end of her baton and pinwheeled her free arm as she tried to keep from falling in the water.

"You've got her going," Finn heard one of her teammates yell over the sound of the wildly cheering crowd. "Push her in!"

Finn pushed harder, but, just as Amy began to fall, she felt her own board start to tip. She pitched forward and held her breath as she hurtled toward the water. Amy went under first, sealing the victory for the '69ers.

"Aren't you glad you played?" Jill asked after Finn and her teammates exchanged high fives.

Finn felt not only victorious. She felt empowered. She hadn't experienced this kind of competitive rush since one of the *Bon Voyage* staff photographers dared her to race against him in a 5K and she'd beaten him by half a mile.

"Same time tomorrow?"

❖

Luisa grew increasingly anxious the closer the time came for her to report to her new post. Would her colleagues ostracize her or welcome her with open arms? She had heard good things about her new commanding officer, but her former one had called her a snitch—and worse—after her efforts to expose his corruption had failed and she had gone over his head to get transferred out of his unit. She had been lucky to latch on to her new job so quickly. But if her tainted reputation had preceded her, she might not last long.

She ironed her uniform pants until the creases were sharp enough to slice through flesh. Then she draped them and her uniform shirt across the back of the couch so they wouldn't wrinkle overnight. She was a decorated soldier and an officer of the Federal Police. When she reported for duty at seven the following morning, she wanted to look the part.

She looked at the clock. Just past seven p.m. Less than twelve hours to go. That was twelve hours too many.

She tried doing push-ups to burn off her nervous energy, but the exercise didn't help. Only one thing could take the edge off: sex. The feel of a woman's body, the heat of her kiss, the warmth of her touch soothed her every time she felt this out of sorts. Since she wasn't seeing anyone, she doubted she would find relief anytime soon. She could have prowled the clubs in the Pink Zone to find companionship for the night, but she didn't want to have sex with just any woman. She wanted to have it with one: Finn.

Luisa picked up the Porky Pig figurine and allowed

reminiscences of Finn to wash over her. What was it about Finn that affected her so? Was it the urgency with which they had come together or the ease with which they had drifted apart? With no regrets and no promises for the future, but blessed with a wealth of memories engendered by an encounter Luisa wouldn't soon forget.

Her phone rang as she watched the lights on the Monument to the Revolution begin to twinkle to life. Unlike last night, this time she paused to check the display. And smiled when she saw the incoming call was from Finn.

"How was your day?" she asked.

"Emotional. I think I've cried three times already."

Luisa turned away from the window, her burst of happiness replaced by dread. "Why? What's wrong?"

"Nothing. Beauty makes me cry. And I've seen several beautiful things today."

"Such as?"

"This morning, I watched a wheelchair-bound woman swim in the Caribbean Sea. This afternoon, I had lunch with a couple who have been together for fifty years but consider themselves newlyweds because they've been legally married for only six months. And now I'm cruising on a yacht, watching the most gorgeous sunset I've ever seen. I wish you were here."

"As beautiful as you make it sound, so do I." Luisa sat on the couch and hugged a throw pillow to her chest. "You seem surprised you're having a good time. Why?"

"When I hear 'tour group,' I automatically picture a bored guide leading a bunch of camera-wielding tourists around at breakneck speed. When they're done, they can say they visited some great places and checked off all the boxes on their to-do lists, but they aren't able to say they had some amazing experiences. This isn't like that."

Luisa was intrigued. "Did you become a travel writer in order to have amazing experiences or to share them with everyone else?"

Finn was silent for a moment. "Both, I guess. No one has ever asked me that before. I suppose they think I do it for the frequent flyer miles."

Luisa had spent the afternoon reading some of Finn's columns online. Articles written in cities large and small, industrial and rural, gentrified and untamed. Even without the accompanying photographs, Luisa had been able to picture where Finn had visited simply by reading her words. Now Finn was here, visiting the country she called home. What words would Finn use to describe her time here? Whatever they were, Luisa couldn't wait to read them.

"Of all the places you've been, which one's your favorite?" she asked.

Finn fell silent again as she pondered the question. Luisa could hear the wind whipping through the phone. She could hear glasses clinking and women laughing in the background. She could hear waves crashing in the distance. She could practically smell the salt air. She wanted to be there, too.

"The best place I've ever been," Finn eventually said, "is in your arms."

Luisa hoped what Finn had said about their time together was more than a come-on. But even if it was, her life was too unsettled for her to be able to pursue a relationship with anyone at the moment but especially someone like Finn—a beautiful butterfly still testing her wings.

"I'm being paged for a group photo," Finn said before Luisa had a chance to respond. "I'd better go before they shanghai me. I'll call you tomorrow, okay?"

"Good night, *mariposa*. I'll be waiting."

Day Three

Finn needed some downtime. She had been "on" for two days now, and the effort she had put into trying to fit in with everyone else instead of setting herself apart from them was exhausting. She placed the Do Not Disturb sign on her door and sat cross-legged on the balcony while she waited for a pot of coffee to brew in the small in-room coffeemaker. The sun was just starting to rise, and the resort was quiet, save a few early risers—runners who wanted to get a few miles in before the temperature got too hot, a bird tweeting its heart out as it tried to attract a mate, and a stingray patrolling the lagoon like a silent sentry.

Finn loved this time of day. When everything was quiet and still. It was one of the few times she came close to feeling the same way.

She took a deep breath and slowly released it as she tried to center herself. Her social anxiety was kicking in again. Her case wasn't as debilitating as others' were. She could function normally as long as she controlled her fear. But she could always tell when she needed to take a break from the world and made sure to heed the signs. If she didn't, she felt like she was being judged and found wanting.

It had started when she was seven. When her childhood stutter had evolved from a cute quirk into a full-blown impediment. Middle school had been pure hell. She had gone out of her way to avoid talking to people because she hadn't known from one encounter to the next if she would be able to get the words out. It had been impossible to remain silent in class, however. When it was her turn to read aloud, her throat would close up, her hands would start to shake, and her body temperature would spike like she was a menopausal woman having a hot flash instead of a sixth-grader trying to plow through a few paragraphs on caste systems in civics class.

She could still hear the snickers of her classmates as she tried to force her faulty mouth, tongue, and throat to work. She remembered her so-called peers' taunts in the hallway and their singsong chants of the nickname she hated. They called her Woody Woodpecker because her staccato efforts to speak reminded them of the cartoon character's distinctive laugh. That laugh had shadowed her for years. Haunted her dreams.

Because speaking was such an issue, she had turned to writing in order to express herself. Diary entries at first, then poems, and eventually, short stories. Writing had allowed her to be anyone she wanted. A rock star. A superhero. Someone famous. Or, more often than not, simply someone normal. In other words, everything she wasn't.

She had longed to go somewhere else. To be someone else. She had dreamed of moving away and becoming a writer one day. To make a living doing what she loved most. But she had never thought her dream would come to pass. Her teachers had praised her fledgling creative efforts and encouraged her to continue to hone her skills. Their positive input had eventually given her the confidence boost she needed to leave her small hometown behind and forge a new path. The path she was still treading today.

Her stutter had gradually disappeared over time as years of speech therapy and a continued use of rhythmic control and slow speech helped to eradicate the disorder. By her senior year of high school, her stutter had practically disappeared. Now she stumbled over her words only when she was nervous or extremely tired. But she never forgot all those frustrating years she had spent as the butt of countless cruel jokes.

Each time she met someone new or found herself immersed in a crowd, she feared she would turn into that scared little girl again. The one who had felt broken for so long. Talk therapy and antidepressants were recommended treatments for her phobia, but she didn't need to pop pills or talk to a shrink to improve her ability to interact with others. She used some of the same techniques she used to control her stutter: relaxation and breathing exercises. When those failed, all she needed to make things right was a ticket to her next destination and a chance to explore it at her own pace.

She rubbed the small tattoo of Woody Woodpecker on the inside of her left ankle. Her attempt to repurpose something that had once been used to put her down and make her feel small. Now the image gave her strength instead of taking it away. Because it reminded her that the life she had now was far better than the one she had left behind.

She took another deep breath, stretched, and got up to pour herself a cup of coffee. As she sipped the strong brew, she wondered how Luisa would react if she knew about her past. Would Luisa be empathetic or would she turn tail and run?

When she told people about her speech disorder, some were overly sympathetic, and most opted to take the inspirational route by giving her a list of famous people in history who had overcome their impediments to do great things. Actor James Earl Jones, Prime Minister Winston Churchill, King George VI, and so on and so on.

Finn had finally stopped mentioning it because she didn't want to become an object of fascination. She didn't want to play the waiting game during a conversation. Her listener waiting for her to stumble over her words while she prayed she wouldn't.

"The fantasy is always better than the reality," she said under her breath as she watched the sky turn from gray to pale blue.

Except she couldn't quite manage to convince herself to believe it. Not this time. Because being with Luisa, even for a few hours, had felt like a dream come true. And she didn't want the dream to end.

❖

Luisa was going to be late for work. A regrettable occurrence on most occasions, but an absolute no-no on her first day. She had left her apartment with plenty of time to spare, but Ines Villalobos, her neighbor across the hall, had cornered her before she could make it to the stairs.

She had seen Mrs. Villalobos peeking at her through the peephole in her reinforced door when she moved in on Saturday, but the elderly woman hadn't tried to start a conversation then. She had waited until Luisa didn't have time to talk instead. Now she wouldn't shut up.

"I saw you moving all those big boxes up the stairs a few days ago," Mrs. Villalobos said. "You're stronger than you look. But why didn't you have your boyfriend or your husband do some of the heavy lifting for you?"

"I'm not married, Mrs. Villalobos."

The old woman's thinning gray eyebrows shot up inquisitively. "Are you spending time with anyone?"

"No." Luisa glanced at her watch. She didn't have time to apologize for the terseness of her response or to go into more detail. She needed to get to work. Her hopes of making a favorable first impression were fading fast.

"You'd be perfect for my grandson, Javier. Come on. I'll show you his picture while we share a morning coffee."

Luisa had picked up her weapons and uniform on Saturday so she wouldn't have to perform the time-consuming tasks today. Now the only obstacle in her path was a talkative octogenarian trying to play matchmaker.

"Some other time. I really must be going."

"Nonsense." Mrs. Villalobos latched ont o Luisa's arm with surprising strength and pulled her inside the apartment. "There's always time for coffee. Have a seat while I pour you a cup."

Luisa sighed in defeat as Mrs. Villalobos ambled toward the kitchen. The woman reminded her of her paternal grandmother, may she rest in peace. Small in stature but endowed with an indomitable will. A silver-haired spitfire whose deeply lined face belied an impish sense of humor.

While Mrs. Villalobos puttered in the kitchen, Luisa looked around the living room.

The furniture was clean and relatively new. The overstuffed cushion on the armchair in front of the TV had already molded itself to match the shape of its diminutive owner. The chair in front of the window was similarly branded. Luisa suspected the perches allowed Mrs. Villalobos the perfect vantage points to keep track of what was happening both in the world at large and closer to home.

Potted plants lined the windowsill, their trailing vines curling toward the floor like a floral waterfall. Nearby, several candles, trinkets, and amulets arranged on a semicircular table formed a shrine to Our Lady of Guadalupe, the patron saint of Mexico.

Luisa reflexively crossed herself, then turned her attention to the dozens of photographs lining the walls. The oldest had turned sepia with age. In the photos, Mrs. Villalobos aged from a fresh-faced bride to the wizened woman she was today. Her children, grandchildren, and great-grandchildren populated the other pictures.

"That's Javier." Mrs. Villalobos set a cup and saucer on the side table next to the broken-in armchair and pointed a gnarled finger at a photograph of a smiling young man with a bowl haircut, delicate features, and gentle eyes framed by long, curling eyelashes. "He's a good boy. Smart, trustworthy, and good with his hands. He owns and operates a souvenir stand near Chichén Itzá. All the items he sells are hand-carved and only one dollar. Practically free."

"Did he make those?" Luisa indicated the string of wooden animals lined up on the coffee table. A lion, a leopard, and a jaguar, the creature their Mayan ancestors revered the most.

"Yes, he did. Those, too." Mrs. Villalobos pointed to the wooden masks adorning one wall. "He makes good money in his souvenir stand. Tourists love his work. Would you like to meet him?"

Luisa nearly choked on her coffee.

"Too hot?"

"No, too much tequila." Luisa waved her hand in front of her mouth to douse the flames.

"I must have given you my cup. I take a little nip of Don Julio each morning to get my heart started. At my age, I need all the help I can get."

If Luisa had to take another sip of the potent brew, she thought her heart might stop altogether. Mrs. Villalobos switched cups, took a sip of the spiked coffee, and sighed in satisfaction.

"That's better." She eyed the insignia on Luisa's uniform shirt. "Now tell me what a nice girl like you is doing getting mixed up with the Federal Police."

"You don't approve?"

Mrs. Villalobos pursed her thin lips. "It seems like dangerous work for a woman."

Luisa had grown immune to the arguments of pigheaded men who tried to convince her she would be happier barefoot and pregnant instead of chasing bad guys, but she couldn't understand the reasoning of women who felt the same way. No matter how old or set in their ways they might be.

She placed the cup and saucer on the coffee table and pushed herself off the lavender-scented couch. "Thank you for the coffee, Mrs. Villalobos," she said, resting her hand on the Glock holstered to her hip, "but I have to get to work."

"Come back when you can stay longer." Mrs. Villalobos followed her to the door, her huarache-clad feet shuffling across the brightly colored area rug. "I'll have to have you over for dinner some night. I could make *chilaquiles* and invite Javier so you two can get to know each other. Javier loves my cooking. If things work out between you, I'll give you my recipes."

"Don't worry about it, Mrs. Villalobos. I'm not much of a cook."

"No? Then how do you expect to catch a man?"

"Through good police work."

Sweat dampened the collar of Luisa's black uniform shirt after she ran down the four flights of stairs and jogged to the parking garage under her apartment building to retrieve her car. She locked the duffel bag containing her AR-15 A3 Tactical Carbine battle rifle and her Heckler & Koch MP5 submachine gun in the trunk and slid into the driver's seat.

Morning traffic was just starting to pick up as she made

her way to the Federal Police Building. When she was in high school, her history teacher used to say, "If you're on time, you're already late." She would definitely earn one of Mr. Montez's infamous rebukes today, but she took a minute to pull herself together before she walked into the glass and steel accented building. She had swept her hair up into a loose bun to keep it off her collar as the uniform regulations dictated. She ran a hand over it to make sure no loose tendrils had worked their way free. Satisfied she was in line with the dress code, she tightened her grip on her duffel bag, took a deep breath, and stepped inside.

She showed her badge to the guard just inside the door. "Officer Luisa Moreno. I have a meeting with Director Chavez."

The guard waved her forward. "Check your weapons with me. I'll return them after I compare the serial numbers to the ones on my list." Luisa handed over her service weapon and duffel bag. "Walk through the metal detector. These will be waiting for you on the other side."

Luisa walked through the machine designed to prevent unauthorized weapons from entering the building.

"Here are your weapons," another guard said after Luisa passed through the metal detector without incident. "Go see the receptionist at the front desk."

"Thank you." Luisa tried not to rush as she headed for the desk, behind which a plump woman wearing half-moon glasses held court. "I'm Officer Luisa Moreno. I have a seven o'clock meeting with Director Chavez."

The receptionist lowered her chin and stared at Luisa over the top of her glasses after taking a pointed look at the clock suspended on the far wall.

"You're late. Director Chavez is a busy man. In the future,

please exhibit a bit more respect for his schedule than you did today."

"I intend to."

"See that you do." The receptionist punched some keys on her computer and spoke into her headset. "Luisa Moreno to see you, sir." She listened for a moment, nodded, and said, "Director Chavez will see you now. He's in the Anti-Drug unit on the—"

"I know where it is. Thank you," Luisa said as she rushed toward the elevator.

"Officer Moreno," the receptionist said in a singsong voice while Luisa frantically pressed the Up button.

"Yes, ma'am?"

When Luisa turned around, the receptionist's pinched glare of disapproval had been replaced by a warm smile.

"Good luck. It would be nice to have another woman around here."

Luisa stepped into the elevator and nodded her thanks before the doors slid shut. She pushed one of the numbered buttons, and the elevator car began to rise. The Scientific Division, the Department of Federal Forces, the Center for Intelligence, and several more federal agencies were housed in the building, but she was headed for one of the most harried—the Anti-Drug Division, whose personnel were tasked with combating drug-related crime.

Luisa felt giddy, her nerves offset by adrenaline. When the elevator doors opened onto a floor bustling with activity, she felt like she was exactly where she belonged.

Arturo Chavez, a barrel-chested man with thick black hair and a mustache like Tom Selleck's circa *Magnum, P.I.*, stepped forward to greet her.

"Director Chavez." Luisa dropped her duffel and snapped

off a crisp salute. "Officer Luisa Moreno reporting for duty, sir."

"Let's dispense with the formalities and head into my office so we can talk in private."

The other officers watched her—some openly, some surreptitiously—as she followed Director Chavez to his office and he closed the door behind them. Exactly the kind of lukewarm welcome she was expecting.

"Before we begin, I apologize for being late, sir, and I assure you it won't happen again."

"I'm sure it won't." Director Chavez leaned back in his leather chair, his dark eyes examining her face. "I've spoken to several people about you, Officer Moreno. Some sang your praises. Others were rather harsh in their criticisms. Tell me whom I should choose to believe."

"Let your eyes be the judge. I wouldn't be on the force if I couldn't do the job. And I wouldn't be sitting here in front of you if I didn't think I could excel at it."

His deep rumble of a belly laugh sounded like a yawning grizzly bear waking up from hibernation.

"I've seen your file, Moreno. I know what you can do. You don't need to prove yourself to me. But you do need to prove yourself to the people outside that door." He pointed toward the officers who had eyed her with a mixture of suspicion and distrust. "They want to bring down the narcos as much as you do, if not more, but they need to know you're willing to be a team player, not a one-woman army. I advise you not to let your dedication lead to recklessness. Doing so could get you or someone else killed. I trust my people. If one was dirty, I would know it even before they did. Understood?"

"Yes, sir. I'm not looking to point fingers at anyone. I just want to do my job."

Director Chavez nodded in apparent agreement. "That's

why the narcos are gunning for you. None of them have officially ordered a hit on you, as far as I know, but it's too dangerous for me to put you on the street until I know for sure."

"Are you asking me to chain myself to a desk?" Luisa couldn't think of a worse punishment.

"I'm asking you to put your investigative skills to work so you can do what your predecessor couldn't: help me identify the leader of the Jaguars so I can put him away and rip his organization apart before he takes over the whole country."

Carlos Ramos was the man whom Luisa had been hired to replace. He had disappeared under mysterious circumstances several months ago, but his body had never been found. Some said he had taken a payoff from the Jaguars and gone into hiding. Others theorized he had been kidnapped and murdered for getting too close to uncovering the Jaguars' secrets. Luisa didn't know him well enough to ascertain which scenario was more likely to be true, but she did know one thing for sure: she didn't plan on following in his tragic footsteps.

"Will you help me bring down the Jaguars?" Director Chavez asked.

"Sir, it would be my honor."

❖

Finn squeezed past the dancers and mariachi singers warming up for tonight's Cinco de Mayo celebration and headed to the front desk in the lobby so she could open a resort account. The gift shop, spa, and excursion office didn't accept cash or credit cards. Everything had to be paid for via an internal account guests set up by tying a credit card to their key card.

Finn handed her credit card to Sebastian, the resort

employee on duty, and watched as he ran a four-hundred-dollar authorization.

"Sign here, please," Sebastian said after he returned her ID, credit card, and key card. Finn balked when she saw five thousand dollars printed on the receipt until she realized the authorization had been run in pesos instead of dollars. "Thanks. You're all set."

Finn slipped her cards into her pocket. She'd stash her ID and credit card in the safe in her room later. She needed to get to the excursion office before it closed. She had missed out on today's trip to Chichén Itzá because she had gotten dragged into a welcome luncheon for first-time SOS Tours travelers. Thursday was the last day the trip would be offered this week. If she didn't make it to the office today, the roster might fill up before she had a chance to add her name to the list.

On her way through the main bar, she noticed a long line in front of the How to Make the Perfect Margarita station. Aurora waved her over.

"Are the drinks really that good?" Finn asked. "It's standing room only in here."

"They are the bomb, but they're also the only game in town. The bartenders, towel girls, servers, maids, security guards, and groundskeepers are on strike. They walked off the job half an hour ago. Brilliant strategy, really. The hotel's completely full. If the manager wants to keep the guests happy, he has no choice but to cave to the employees' demands. This disruption had better not last long. Otherwise, we'll have to fend for ourselves."

"We're lesbians," Finn said. "We're used to that. The police officers in attendance can handle security; the doctors, nurses, and paramedics can run the infirmary. I haven't run into a bartender yet, but I'm sure we could find plenty of volunteers to fill the position."

"What can you do?"

As she mentally ran through the list of jobs that would need to be done in the workers' absence, Finn realized she wasn't qualified to fill most of them. Her skills were creative, not practical.

"I'm only good for providing comic relief." Often at her own expense. "Or maybe I could be the staff photographer."

"Every lesbian with a digital camera wants that job," Aurora said, "me included. Think about it. You spend three months in paradise—or however long these gigs usually last before the resort owners ship you off to your next assignment. You wander around taking pictures of beautiful, half-dressed tourists all day, put the pictures in a keepsake package, and sit back while people pay you through the nose for capturing their vacation memories while they were having too much fun to do it for themselves. Girl, we got this. The workers can strike as long as they want."

"When life hands you lemons, make lemonade, right?"

"I'd prefer a lemon drop martini, but to each her own. And this will do in a pinch." Aurora took a sip from her salt-rimmed glass. "It's five o'clock somewhere."

"But hopefully not here," Finn said. "I need to get to the excursion office before it closes. Or are they on strike, too?"

"The excursion group has a separate contract with the hotel. You should be fine. Which trip are you thinking about signing up for?"

Finn had passed by the excursion office so many times as she wandered through the resort over the past three days she had practically memorized the group's offerings. The jungle adventure that included a climb to the top of the tallest Mayan monument in the Yucatán Peninsula, followed by lunch on the beach in Tulum, and a swim in an underground river. The trip to the ancient city of Ek' Balam, the capital of the former Talol kingdom. The lobster cruise to Isla Mujeres. The shopping excursion to Playa del Carmen in the heart of the Mayan Riviera. And so on and so on.

"I want to see the pyramids in Chichén Itzá. They're considered one of the Seven Wonders of the modern world."

She had never seen the pyramids in person and, since the editors of *Bon Voyage* didn't like to explore the same area twice, she didn't know when or if she would have the chance again.

"It's now or never," she said to herself as she pushed the glass door open and walked into the excursion office.

"How may I help you today?" a woman with curly brown hair and a French accent asked as she rooted through a box of pamphlets advertising the "once-in-a-lifetime" opportunity to swim with dolphins in a nearby aquarium. Her name tag read Veronique.

"I want to sign up for Thursday's trip to Chichén Itzá. It's not full, is it?"

"Almost, but I think we have room for one more. Let me check the list. We limit these trips to a maximum of forty people in the interest of time and space, but I think we have—" She ran her finger down a handwritten list of names and room numbers. "Thirty-nine," she announced with a gap-toothed grin. "Like I said. Room for one more. The trip is fifteen hundred pesos. If you've set up an account with the hotel, give me your room key and we'll get started."

While Veronique swiped her card in the small reader hooked to her computer terminal, Finn added her name and room number to the manifest. Then she listened attentively as Veronique told her how to prepare for her upcoming trip.

"Chichén Itzá is located near the jungle, so the weather will be very hot and humid. That's why we offer the trip early in the day. Later in the afternoon, the conditions are too brutal for the outing to be enjoyable. You will have a six a.m. wake-up call on Thursday, and the main restaurant will open an hour early so you and your fellow travelers can have breakfast before you leave. The bus will depart promptly at seven and will return at two thirty that afternoon. Be sure to wear comfortable shoes because there will be a great deal of walking. There isn't much shade. Sunscreen, sunglasses, and a hat are highly recommended, as is mosquito repellent. Bring a camera so you can take plenty of pictures, and cash if you want to purchase souvenirs. There are many available at the site, and the bus will stop at a small indoor flea market on the way so you can look around or simply stretch your legs. Lunch is not included, but you are welcome to bring snacks of your own. The bus is air-conditioned and it has its own bathroom, which might come in handy since the pyramids are two hours away. Do you have any questions?"

"Yes. Who's the guide? Is it someone from the area?" Finn wanted to learn something only locals knew, not something she could read in a brochure.

"All our guides are local and are extremely knowledgeable about their selected routes. Your guide will be Richard Haarhuis. He's from Amsterdam originally, but he has lived in Mexico for several years and is married to a Mexican national. He has a personal connection to and a true affinity for Mayan culture. He's one of our best and most popular guides."

"Excellent."

"Will that be all or do you see something else that interests you?"

Finn couldn't tell if Veronique meant the excursions or her.

"That's all for now. Thanks for your help."

"Anytime. I'm here all week if you change your mind."

Finn left the office and headed for the beach. She had

experienced her share of flings and one-night stands while she was on assignment, but she was only slightly tempted to add Veronique to the list. Even though Veronique was incredibly attractive and her accent was beyond sexy, she didn't hold a candle to Luisa. At the moment, no one else could compare. Finn looked forward to their daily phone calls and the fantasy-fueled nights that followed.

Her favorite fantasy featured Luisa wearing nothing but her gun belt and a set of handcuffs. She had never been a huge fan of bondage, but Officer Luisa Moreno could shackle her any time she wanted.

Today was Luisa's first day at work. Finn wondered how it had gone. She hoped Luisa would tell her about it later. If, that was, she was allowed to talk about it. The goings-on inside the Federal Police Building were confidential, so Luisa was probably sworn to secrecy.

Finn had never dated a cop before. But was that what she and Luisa were doing, dating? Sex usually came after the getting-to-know-you stage, not before. Yet another first Finn could chalk up to this trip.

"At this rate, my bucket list will be empty in two days."

She hoped she hadn't scared Luisa off by responding to her question the way she had. Luisa probably hadn't expected to hear her say her favorite location was in Luisa's arms. Finn hadn't expected to say it, either, but she couldn't deny that it was true. Or that she wanted to be there again. Right now, in fact.

What was it Luisa had called her before they ended last night's call? *Mariposa*. Butterfly. Finn had never been compared to the delicate creatures that brought such beauty to the world. Though she didn't know if the comparison was apt, she loved the idea that Luisa thought she was beautiful. Or that

Luisa continued to think of her at all, given the brevity of their meeting and the abruptness of their parting.

Could they build a future on such an unsteady foundation, or were Finn's postcard-perfect surroundings trying to fool her into thinking she could live her own version of happily ever after?

A serious reality check was in order. Easier said than done when she was spending the week in paradise, surrounded by singles hoping to fall in love and couples who were already there.

She looked at several pairs of women holding hands as they made their way to the manicured garden for a mass commitment ceremony. In America, gay marriage was finally legal in all fifty states, but there were still a few holdouts internationally. Many countries had adopted laws in favor of marriage equality, but many more refused to do so. For the women living under those circumstances, today's ceremony might be as close as they would ever come to getting married.

Finn never cried at weddings, but she felt herself start to tear up as she watched the women look into their respective partners' eyes and pledge to love one another until the end of their days. How did it feel to have a connection that ran that deep? She had heard that falling in love was much easier than remaining that way. How much work did it take to make love last? More than she was willing to put in at this point in her life, that was for sure.

Feeling more like an intruder than an observer, Finn walked away as the commitment ceremony neared its conclusion.

Same-sex marriage was legal in Mexico City and civil unions were recognized throughout the country. Did Luisa want to get married one day? Did she want to start a family of her own? Did she want all the things Finn had never considered, or did she realize her job was too dangerous for her to plan a future she might not live to see?

"Definitely a conversation that would need to take place in person, not over the phone," Finn said under her breath as she sat on an empty lounge chair on the beach and watched parasailers float across the cloudless sky.

The familiar choruses of "Would you like something to drink?" echoing around her signaled the employee strike had come to an end.

"The booze is back," someone said. "All is right with the world."

In their world, perhaps. In Finn's, everything had been turned upside down. She didn't know which end was up. Did she want to continue living life on her own and on her own terms, or did she want to share her life with someone? Namely, someone like Luisa Moreno.

A smiling waitress wearing a sky blue polo shirt and crisp white cotton shorts came over to her, drink tray in hand. "Would you like something, ma'am?"

"Yeah. Answers."

❖

Luisa's eyes were crossing. She had spent the morning taking care of all the administrative legwork that came with a new position—completing reams of paperwork for Human Resources, obtaining user IDs and passwords for the computer systems from the guys in IT, and testing her access codes to the rooms her security clearance allowed her to enter. After lunch, she had gathered Carlos Ramos's old case files and begun looking through them, searching for clues to the direction his investigation of the Jaguars had been headed before he vanished. She had examined dozens of crime scene photographs and read hundreds of pages of reports, but she was no closer to unraveling the twin mysteries of Ramos's disappearance and the identity of the leader of the Jaguars cartel. She was so tired she couldn't see straight, but she didn't want to stop until she felt like she had made some progress.

Director Chavez came out of his office carrying a battered briefcase that had seen better days. He paused in front of Luisa's desk.

"You're not getting paid by the hour, Moreno. Just because you came in late doesn't mean you have to stay late."

Luisa looked at the time stamp on the corner of her computer screen. No wonder she was so tired. It was past seven o'clock. She had been working for nearly twelve hours. "I'm almost done, sir. One more file and I'll call it a day."

"Have at it then." He tossed a wave over his shoulder as he headed for the elevator.

Luisa stood, stretched, and looked around at the rest of the stragglers. At least ten other people were putting in a late night, too. She locked her computer and headed to the bathroom to splash some water on her face. Her stomach's insistence on food overrode her desire to keep working. She decided to go home and start fresh in the morning.

When she returned to her desk, a rubber rat rested on her computer monitor. The note taped to the rat's belly read, "You can sit at Carlos Ramos's desk, but you can't fill his shoes. The real enemy is outside, not within these walls. Protect your own, and they will protect you. Turn on your own, and no one will be around to hear you fall."

She looked around the room to see who might claim responsibility for the note or give themselves away by their reaction to watching her find it, but no one was brave enough to meet her eye. She wanted to yell at the top of her lungs that breaking the code of silence didn't make her a snitch. That trying to limit the narcos' influence didn't make her a rat. But she knew trying to defend herself would do no good. The ones who thought she was a traitor to the ranks would continue to think that way. As would the ones who thought the only reason she had spoken up was to advance her career at a respected colleague's expense. She couldn't change people's opinions of her in one day—and she couldn't take down the Jaguars in one afternoon. So she resolved to come back the next day and start all over again.

She tossed the rat in the trash, shut her computer down, and gathered her belongings with as much dignity as she could muster.

"I don't think I'm better than you." She tried to keep her voice from shaking so no one could tell how much the hazing had affected her. "I just want to be one of you. Tomorrow, I hope you give me a chance to do just that. Good night."

She managed to maintain her composure until she reached the safety of her car. Then she allowed her façade to fall, along with her tears.

❖

Finn's call to Luisa's cell phone went straight to voice mail. Again. She listened as the automated message played.

"You have reached Luisa Moreno," Luisa's voice said in Spanish. "I am unable to come to the phone right now. Please leave your name and number, and I will call you back as soon as I can."

Finn was more comfortable translating Spanish than speaking it so she left her message—her third—in English.

"Hey, Luisa, it's Finn. I hope I don't seem stalkerish, but I've been calling you all night and I haven't been able to reach you. I'm starting to get worried. I was hoping to hear how your day was. Now I'm just hoping to hear from you at all. I hope I'm overreacting. I hope you're simply working late and have your phone turned off. If that's the case, we can laugh about it later. But in the meantime, call me. Please."

She ended the call and looked at the clock. It was past midnight. She had been trying to call Luisa for five hours with no luck.

"Perhaps I should take the hint."

Maybe Luisa hadn't returned her calls because she didn't want to, not because she couldn't. Their first few conversations had been light and fun, but the last one had taken a serious turn near the end. Maybe, as Finn had feared that morning, her words had scared Luisa away. But Luisa didn't seem like the type of woman who scared easily. In fact, she might be too brave for her own good.

Finn stepped onto the balcony outside her room, but the insistent thump-thump-thump of the dance music playing at the outdoor disco drove her back inside.

Was this what it was like to date a cop? Sentenced to sleepless nights waiting for the phone to ring while part of you hoped it wouldn't for fear it might be bad news? If so, she wasn't sure if she was up to the task.

Her phone finally rang several minutes later. She blew out a sigh of relief when she saw Luisa's name on the display. "How was your day?"

"Long."

Finn frowned. She had tried to keep her tone light, but Luisa sounded distant. Edgy. "Do you want to talk about it?"

"Not really."

"Oh." A few days ago, holding a conversation with Luisa had been easy. Now it was like pulling teeth. Perhaps it was time for her to do what she did best: leave. Before being with Luisa stopped being fun and began to turn into something neither of them seemed to want. "We don't have to do this if you're not into it. I should hang up and call you tomorrow when you're in a better mood, or maybe I should stop calling altogether."

"No. Don't do that." Luisa's voice sounded strangled. Like she was choking back a sob. "Just talk to me, Finn. Make me forget the shitty day I had. Give me reason to believe tomorrow will be better."

Finn wasn't used to being someone's shoulder to cry on. She didn't know how to go about it. She resorted to humor because laughter was supposed to be the best medicine.

"In the immortal words of Scarlett O'Hara, 'Tomorrow is another day.' If you could live this one over, what would you do different?"

Luisa was quiet for a moment, then she let out a rueful laugh. "I wouldn't have wasted fifteen minutes of it listening to my neighbor trying to fix me up with her grandson. Because it was all downhill from there."

Finn could feel Luisa finally begin to relax. She wished she could be there to see the light banish the darkness from Luisa's soulful brown eyes. She wished she could be there to stroke her black hair and hold her close. She wished she could be there. Even though she couldn't be there with her, she could still be there for her.

"When's the wedding?" she asked.

Luisa laughed again. With less of an effort this time. "Never, if I can help it. The grandson's cute, but he's not my type."

"Did you tell your neighbor you were a lesbian?"

"No, but I don't think it would matter. She'd probably trot out the 'you just haven't met the right man' speech and try even harder to hook me up with one."

"Do I need to come out there and protect my interests?"

"You might. Otherwise, I could be Mrs. Javier Villalobos by the time you see me again."

Finn felt uncharacteristically possessive. She wanted to hold on instead of letting go. "When will I see you again?" she said, unable to resist asking the question.

"I wish I knew. Until my probationary period is over, I have to keep my nose to the grindstone. Lots of long days and very little, if any, time off. I would love to play hooky tomorrow and spend the day with you, sipping margaritas on the beach and feeling the sand between my toes, but I can't. I have to be here."

Finn had a feeling that, deep down, Luisa didn't want to be anywhere else.

"Someone's got to catch the bad guys, right?" she asked.

"That's the plan. Unfortunately, it doesn't always work out that way. Sometimes the good guys end up getting caught in the middle."

"Are you going to tell me what happened today?" Finn asked the question reluctantly because she wasn't sure she was ready—or willing—to hear the answer.

"Not if I can help it."

Finn felt Luisa slide toward the gloomy mood she'd been in at the beginning of the call and tried to pull her back.

"Then tell me something else."

"Something like what?"

"Tell me about the first time you kissed a girl."

"It was last Saturday in Dallas."

"Right," Finn said sarcastically. "The way you kissed me, you've obviously had lots of practice. Who gave you your first lesson?"

"I'm sure you're familiar with the term 'kissing cousins.' My cousin, Gabriela, taught me everything I know. When I came out to her years later, she joked I was her first recruit."

"She's a lesbian, too?"

"Yes, but her parents haven't been as accepting as mine. She and I talk all the time, but she hasn't spoken to her parents in several years. When she came out to them, they said they wished she was dead. If they could see some of the images I saw today, I think they would change their minds."

Finn didn't ask Luisa what horrors she had witnessed today. She could imagine all sorts of terrible things, but she was willing to bet reality was exponentially worse.

"What about you?" Luisa asked. "Who gave you your first kiss?"

"Nancy Everhart, one of my classmates. I was in the third grade. We all brought cards to school for Valentine's Day, and we took turns handing them out. When it was her turn, Nancy handed out kisses instead. And not the kind that come in a foil wrapper. She ended up giving me two. One during class and one after."

"Overachiever."

"No, it was quality control. I had to make sure I liked it as much the second time as I did the first."

"Did you?"

"It didn't take me long to become a convert. Let's put it that way."

Nancy had provided one of the few bright spots during that dark time in her life. Finn still remembered the feel of Nancy's lips on hers. Soft. Gentle. Filled with promise. She had always thought it was the sweetest kiss she had ever received. Until she was kissed by Luisa Moreno.

"Now you have five hundred willing practice partners," Luisa said.

"More like seventy-five. The rest are spoken for."

"Have you met anyone you've wanted to practice with?"

Was that a hint of jealousy she heard in Luisa's voice? She liked the sound of it.

"Here? I haven't been looking. I think you spoiled me."

"I would apologize, but if I did, it would be less than genuine."

Finn stared at the moon shining full and bright outside her window, feeling close to Luisa despite the many miles between them.

"What are you doing tomorrow?" Luisa asked, her voice low and almost dreamlike.

"Tomorrow's a bit of a down day, but I'm going to Chichén Itzá on Thursday. Have you ever been?"

"Once. When I was in high school. My history teacher took me and the rest of the class on a field trip."

"What did you think of it?"

"Now, I think it's an amazing architectural achievement. Back then, I was too immature to appreciate it. My friends and I called it Chicken Pizza. We were just happy to be out of school for the day. We didn't care about the history lesson involved."

"I'll try to pay closer attention to the tour guide than you did."

"It won't take much effort on your part, believe me."

Finn liked Luisa's self-deprecating sense of humor. She liked everything else about her, too. All this talk of the past had her feeling like a teenager hiding under the covers talking on the phone with her first crush. God, she could get used to this.

"Do you plan on working late tomorrow, too?" she asked.

Luisa's answering laugh sounded equally amused and exhausted.

"No, but I didn't plan on working late today, either."

"Then why don't you call me instead? If you're up to it, that is."

"I will. And I promise not to wait until midnight to do it. By the way, thanks for being so concerned about me today. You didn't sound stalkerish at all. Is that another word you picked up on the road? It's not even a word at all, is it?"

"It is now." Finn giggled. Luisa quickly joined in. "I hope you have a better day tomorrow."

"I hope so, too."

"Are we going to do this, Luisa, or are we just having fun?"

"I don't know," Luisa said after a moment's pause. "Let's just play it by ear. Good night, *mariposa*."

"Good night, super cop." Finn ended the call, then spoke into the sudden silence. "And make sure to catch the bad guys before they catch you."

Day Four

Luisa locked her apartment door and politely but firmly refused Mrs. Villalobos's offer of a cup of coffee. There was no way she was going to be late for work two days in a row. Especially after the harsh treatment she had received last night. She clenched her teeth at the memory of the fake rat someone had placed on her computer monitor and wondered what her so-called "colleagues" would have in store for her today. Would they use live animals instead of rubber ones, or would they escalate to slashing her tires or smashing her windshield? No wonder Director Chavez was reluctant to put her on the street. With things the way they were now, she might end up getting gunned down by the people who were supposed to be on her side, not the ones she was trying to catch.

If none of Director Chavez's people were dirty, they should have welcomed her into their ranks instead of attempting to exclude her from them. She needed to find a way to win them over. Fast. Solving the mystery of Carlos Ramos's disappearance could go a long way toward currying their favor.

"Are you sure you don't have time for one cup?" Mrs. Villalobos asked. "I'll make sure not to give you the one with the tequila in it today."

"I can't this morning."

Luisa's heart melted when Mrs. Villalobos's face fell. The woman was obviously lonely and probably desperate for company. Just like she was. As much as she liked talking on the phone with Finn every night, the long-distance exchanges weren't nearly as satisfying as they could be if they took place face-to-face. For her, a conversation wasn't complete unless she could look the other person in the eye or lay her hand on them and feel the warmth of their skin. She preferred doing it with a lover, but it was almost as much fun to do it with a friend. Almost.

"Perhaps I can come see you this weekend when I have more time to talk," she said. "We can split a bag of *churros* while we get to know each other better."

Mrs. Villalobos's expression brightened. "It will be nice to have a little girl talk with someone other than myself for a change. Are you free Saturday night as well?"

"What happens then?" Luisa asked warily.

"I have a surprise for you." Based on the twinkle in Mrs. Villalobos's eyes, Luisa had a pretty good idea what the surprise might be. Mrs. Villalobos didn't disappoint her. "I spoke with Javier last night and he's coming to see me this weekend. If you don't have any plans for Saturday night, why don't you join us for dinner? As skinny as you are, you could use more than a bag of *churros*." She pinched Luisa's side like she was trying to find the perfect cut of meat at the local butcher shop. "You need a home-cooked meal or two. Do you like *tamales*?"

Luisa's first instinct was to decline Mrs. Villalobos's invitation because she didn't want to deal with the resulting awkwardness when she revealed the reason why any relationship she might have with Javier would never be anything other than platonic, but she had never been able to resist a big plate of *tamales* smothered in salsa and Oaxaca cheese. "Pork or beef?"

"Both," Mrs. Villalobos said with a wink. "And if I have time, I might bake a *tres leches* cake for dessert."

Luisa could feel her mouth watering already. "It's a date."

"Excellent. I'll call Javier right now. He'll be so pleased to hear you're joining us. I texted him your picture last night. He thinks you're cute."

Luisa resisted asking how Mrs. Villalobos had gotten her picture or obtained the technological know-how to text it to her grandson. The explanation could not only eat into her drive time but also result in an arrest. She didn't want to start her day by handcuffing an eighty-year-old woman and dragging her in for invasion of privacy. She longed for the days when snooping on your neighbor meant peeking at them through the blinds or listening to their arguments through the walls, not snapping unauthorized pictures with a smartphone.

"I'll see you this weekend, Mrs. Villalobos."

"Have a good day, dear. And be careful. Mexico City is a dangerous place. Even for people carrying guns."

"Especially them."

She had lost track of the scores of state, local, and federal authority figures that had been murdered by narcos' hired thugs over the years simply for doing their jobs. Now she might be the next addition to the steadily growing list. The thought frightened her, but inspired her, too. If the narcos wanted her dead, that meant she was getting closer to rooting them out. It remained to be seen who would accomplish their goal first—her or them.

In the parking garage, she performed a quick security sweep of her car to make sure it hadn't been tampered with overnight. Some might call her overly cautious. Some might call her paranoid. They could call her anything they wanted as long as her actions kept her and her loved ones safe.

Once she was satisfied she hadn't become a hit man's target, she drove to the Federal Police Building and let herself inside. After she passed through the security checkpoints, she nodded at Maribel Rodriguez, the receptionist who had given her such a hard time yesterday, and took the elevator upstairs. She expected her reception to be a cool one, so she wasn't surprised by the hostile silence that fell over the room the instant she walked in.

She let out a cheery "Good morning" and sat at her desk when what she really wanted to do was stand on top of it and remind them that the bad guys were supposed to be outside, not in this room. But she couldn't do that with complete confidence until she discovered how many, if any, of her peers were on the cartels' payrolls. As far as she knew, the bad guys could be sitting right next to her.

Picking up where she had left off the night before, she booted up her computer and began poring through Carlos Ramos's case files. Ramos's notes were both prolific and thorough. As she read through them, she could see their author devolve from an idealistic rookie determined to eliminate crime to a jaded veteran officer frustrated by his inability to accomplish his goals. She was tempted to skip to the end of the last file to see what he was thinking right before he disappeared, but she forced herself to read the notes in chronological order so she would be able to make an educated guess about his whereabouts—and an informed decision regarding the conclusions he had drawn about the three main cartels running roughshod over Mexico.

At one time, the Sinaloa cartel, based primarily in Culiacán, was widely considered the world's most powerful money laundering, drug trafficking, and organized crime syndicate.

The group had a presence in seventeen Mexican states, twelve American states, and nine Latin American countries, as well as parts of Europe, Asia, and West Africa, allowing them to ship marijuana, opium, heroin, and methamphetamines around the world.

Until the Jaguars came along, the Sinaloas' only real rivals appeared to be Los Zetas. The Zs were bigger than the Sinaloa cartel in terms of geographic presence—assassinating, kidnapping, and extorting their way to the top of the food chain from their base of operations across the border from Laredo, Texas. They were the violent criminal syndicate US officials once considered the most dangerous, sophisticated, and technologically advanced cartel operating in Mexico. They were well armed and their tactics were brutal. They preferred to torture, behead, and indiscriminately slaughter their enemies, using violence instead of bribery to get what they wanted. They had set up covert camps to train new recruits, which included current and former federal, state, and local police officers from both sides of the border, and their reach was so vast they had been able to entice former US soldiers to traffic drugs, smuggle weapons, or act as hit men on their behalf.

Until they were both overrun by the Jaguars, the Sinaloas and the Zs had fought for supremacy for years, leaving a swath of violence in their wake. Luisa examined the gory evidence of their rise to power. She sifted through glossy photos of mass graves filled with victims both culpable and innocent. Rival gang members who had stood in the cartels' way and ordinary citizens who had dared to resist their growing influence.

She couldn't reconcile herself with the wondrous beauty of her country and the horrible violence that threatened to tear it apart. In Guerrero, the state south of where she now sat, tourists were drawn to the glitz and glamour of Acapulco, while farmers and villagers in the countryside were forced to take up arms and form their own ad hoc police forces in order to combat the cartels that operated openly despite the presence of the military.

The troops, like her former commanding officer, had been paid handsomely to let the cartels do as they pleased. They even warned their benefactors when opposing forces were closing in, allowing the flood of cash and illegal drugs to continue unabated.

Luisa and her friends had grown up cowering in fear from tales about the Sinaloas and the Zs, but—although heinous—the cartels' exploits paled in comparison to the Jaguars'. She referred to Ramos's case notes to bolster what she already knew.

The Jaguars seemed to have eyes everywhere. They were suspected of placing lookouts at airports and bus stations and along main roads so they could keep tabs on people entering and leaving the country. Their main base of operations was along the Gulf of Mexico, a former Los Zetas stronghold, but they had quickly moved south and west, usurping other cartels' territory along the way. They were active in several states north of the border, but they had not managed to invade Europe or Asia. Yet. With the amount of money they were raking in by focusing on local markets, they obviously felt no need to expand.

Luisa remembered a recent raid on a Jaguar safe house in Tabasco that had resulted in the arrest of low-level Jaguars cartel member Hernan Cisneros and the seizure of cash and assets valued at well over five million dollars. Though the amount appeared to be exorbitant, it was thought to represent only a small fraction of the Jaguars' wealth. The raid had created headlines, but it hadn't resulted in a significant hit to the Jaguars' cash flow. And to make matters worse, Cisneros had been killed in prison before he could be persuaded to testify against his fellow cartel members or reveal the identity of the Jaguars' leader.

A prison guard had been arrested and charged for Cisneros's murder. Despite the large cash deposit he had made a few days before the killing, he claimed not to have ties to the Jaguars, though it was widely assumed he had been contracted to ensure the Jaguars' secrets remained intact and their leader's identity remained a mystery. A mystery Luisa—and Carlos Ramos before her—was determined to solve.

Cisneros's death was the latest murder attributed to the Jaguars. The first had not required a similar leap of faith. Their first victim was of one of the Sinaloas' eight plaza bosses, regional leaders who managed the cartel's operations along the Sonora-Arizona corridor and directed the flow of narcotics into the United States. The other seven plaza bosses soon fell. The Zs were initially thought to be to blame until the Jaguars claimed responsibility via a series of letters sent to the largest newspapers in all thirty-one Mexican states.

Investigative journalists had attempted to track the source of the letters, but neither the writer nor the senders had ever been found. Not even after Jaguars hit men began going after the Zs and their allies.

The inner circles of the main cartels were quickly decimated, leaving a sizable hole the Jaguars soon filled. Now their grip on Mexico's lucrative drug trade was as firm as a vise. Their hold on Mexico's citizens was just as tight. Most feared them. Some idolized them. But no one dared to cross them. Not if they wanted to live.

Luisa closed her eyes, but was unable to block out the images of the Jaguars' victims. Images of men, women, and children with their throats slit, their bodies riddled with bullets, and identifying features such as their hands, feet, and teeth removed danced in her mind's eye. One detail nagged at her. In a handful of the photos, some of the victims had had a small rectangular flap of skin removed from their forearms. Ramos's notes revealed he thought it was a particular hit man's calling card, but perhaps it was something else. Perhaps the action was not meant to identify the person who had pulled the trigger, but to obscure the identities of the victims. Were they connected in some way? If so, what did they have in common?

Had they been targeted by hit men working for the Jaguars, or were they Jaguars trigger men who had been killed by the opposition? If a rival cartel had committed the murders, they had yet to claim responsibility for them, an unprecedented move in a war fueled by hubris and testosterone.

The first thing Luisa needed to do was identify the four unnamed victims. One had "The World is My Barrio" tattooed in elaborate scripted letters across his stomach. Ramos's notes indicated he had run an image of the tattoo through a database that tracked prisoners' ink after they passed through intake, but Luisa couldn't find a record of the result. She accessed the database she needed, pasted a copy of the image into the program, and ran the test again. The tattoo quickly came back as a match to Salvador Perez, who was currently serving five years in Santa Martha, notorious for both its overcrowding and its violence. His tattoo was an exact match to the dead man's, but the corpse was estimated to belong to someone between thirty and forty years of age. Salvador Perez was only nineteen. Too young to be a contemporary of the dead man, but old enough to pay tribute to his dubious legacy.

Perez's mother, Silvia, was listed as his primary contact. No phone number was provided, and her address was in the tiny village of Agua Dulce, some four hundred miles away. Perhaps a road trip was in order. Luisa would start with Salvador and, if necessary, drive to Agua Dulce to pay his mother a visit. She called the warden at Santa Martha to set up an appointment for later that afternoon.

"You look like you could use a break."

Luisa looked up to find Ruben Huerta from Records Management standing in front of her desk. Slight, bespectacled, and prematurely balding, he was in charge of cataloguing and storing current and former case files. He gave her the third degree every time she asked for access to something from the archives, though she couldn't decide if he was being thorough, possessive, territorial, or all three.

"May I buy you a burrito?" he asked.

After a day and a half of being iced out by most of her coworkers, Luisa was surprised to see one make a concerted—and very public—effort to invite her into the fold. Or was Ruben attempting to lure her into a trap? She was too hungry to care, and if it came down to it, she thought she could take him in a fight. He didn't look strong enough to stay upright during a stiff breeze, let alone withstand an assault from someone trained in hand-to-hand combat.

"Sounds good to me."

She locked her computer, pushed her chair away from her desk, and followed Ruben to Salon Corona. The restaurant was founded in the 1920s, but the dining area resembled a cocktail lounge from the 1970s. Despite the garish decorations, the food was good and the spot was a lunchtime favorite with the people who worked in or near the center of town.

"You seem surprised," Ruben said after they placed their orders. "Were you expecting me to take you to a cheap *taquería* instead?"

"To be honest, I didn't know what to expect." Luisa spread her napkin in her lap. "I still don't."

Ruben pushed his glasses up on the bridge of his aquiline nose, but they quickly slipped back down to the pointed tip.

"Are you always this suspicious?"

Luisa angled her chair so she was facing the door instead of sitting with her back to it. She wasn't expecting anything to happen in such a public place and in front of so many potential witnesses, but if it did, she wanted to see it coming instead of getting caught by surprise.

"It's what makes me a good police officer."

"Being a good police officer could also get you killed."

"Is that what happened to Carlos Ramos?"

Ruben's eyes widened behind his thick corrective lenses, and he nearly choked on the complimentary chips and salsa the waitress had brought out shortly after they were seated.

"I could speculate about what happened to Carlos," he said, taking a sip of water, "but no one knows for sure. Have you found anything in the case files that might lead you to his whereabouts?"

Luisa leaned back in her seat to give the waitress room to place her loaded chicken burrito and side of guacamole on the table. Despite the presence of the fragrant food and boisterous diners, the outing was starting to feel less like lunch and more like a fishing expedition.

She had discovered a few potential leads that hadn't already been released to the public—such as the missing flap of skin on the four unidentified murder victims' forearms—but some were years old, and she wouldn't be able to determine how promising they might turn out to be until she followed up on them. She decided to keep that information to herself, however. She couldn't risk having her nascent investigation compromised—by internal or external forces.

"Not yet, but I'm working on it."

Ruben's burrito weighed more than he did, but he devoured half of it before Luisa had taken more than a couple bites of hers.

"I, for one, am rooting for you," he said, reaching for more chips and salsa. "Carlos Ramos was a good man. He didn't deserve what happened to him." The sentiment held an air of certainty Ruben probably didn't intend to reveal because he immediately backtracked from his statement. "Whatever that might turn out to be, of course."

Luisa was tempted to ask him what he knew, but she didn't want to be too obvious and scare away a potential source—or possible suspect. She took a sip of her bottled water to give Ruben time to burn off his nervousness but pressed forward before he could get too comfortable.

"Do you think it's more likely Ramos was paid off or rubbed out?"

Ruben frowned like she had besmirched the dead man's honor. "Like I said, Carlos was a good man. I know his family. I knew him. We grew up in the same town." His voice shook with emotion, revealing ties that were personal, not just professional. "He wasn't dirty. He was trying to get at the truth. In the end, I think the truth found him."

The irony of Ruben's words didn't escape Luisa. The truth was supposed to set you free, but it might have gotten Carlos Ramos killed. And if she weren't careful, she could very well be next.

"I'll make a deal with you," Ruben said. "I'm so far out of the loop in Records, I'm usually the last to know anything. But if I see or hear something you can use, I promise to share it with you."

Luisa deliberately kept her expression blank so she wouldn't betray either her excitement or her lingering doubts.

"What would you expect from me in return?"

"I want you to catch the bastards that most likely killed my friend."

Luisa had been trained to tell when a suspect was lying to

her. She examined Ruben's face and body language for telltale signs he was being less than honest but found none. She tossed her napkin on the table and extended her hand.

"You've got a deal."

❖

Finn checked the schedule. The day's agenda was pretty light, most likely geared toward allowing the people who had signed up for optional excursions to feel like they weren't missing out on something by being away from the hotel for hours on end. The pool games had just ended. She and the five members of her team had piled themselves on the same surfboard one by one and maneuvered it around the pool using only their arms and legs to propel them. They had finished a distant second to a bunch of ringers who had obviously played the game before. That was her excuse, anyway, and she was sticking to it.

With the pool games over for the day, her options for the rest of the afternoon included sitting through a presentation on SOS Tours' upcoming vacations, taking a dance lesson in the fitness center, or trying her hand at speed dating on the beach. She could get a list of next year's scheduled trips on SOS's website, she already knew how to dance, and she still had nightmares from the last time she had tried to impress someone in sixty seconds or less. To save herself from further shame, she decided to take a walk on the beach in the hopes of capturing a few photographs to accompany her upcoming article and to see if she could make it from one end to the other before the tide rolled in.

The beach was narrower than she expected. The part closest to the water was hard-packed and easier to walk on, but the sharp angle made keeping her balance tricky. That left the soft-packed sand, which made for slow going and gave her a serious workout. Her calves and thighs were burning in no time. Perfect since her arms and shoulders were still numb from the thirty minutes she had spent trying to paddle a lesbian-laden surfboard around the pool.

"I used to think I was in pretty good shape until I started trying to keep up with these women."

They not only partied hard. They played that way, too.

After she took a picture of two women walking hand in hand in the surf, she thumbed through some of the images she had already captured on her digital camera. The earliest photos she had taken after she arrived in Cancún were of her room, the hotel, and the surrounding grounds.

It was easier for her to focus on landscapes and animals rather than people. Money shots for the magazine subscribers who were as addicted to travel porn as she was.

The pictures of iguanas sunning themselves on the sidewalk and bath towels folded to look like cranes gradually gave way to more personal images. Jill pensively staring at the sea from her perch on a beachside cabana. Aurora floating in the water while her handlers held her aloft. Katie leading a group of Indies through a game of Twister during Happy Hour at the seafront bar. Sasha learning to fly on the trapeze as she rehearsed for tomorrow night's amateur circus.

Finn felt a connection to these women. These five hundred strangers who were starting to feel like lifelong friends. Some were marginalized at home and weren't able to be out year-round. But for this week at least, they were finally, utterly free.

Finn shook her head, marveling at how far the gay rights movement had come over the years—and how many strides still needed to be made. But she was proud to find herself in the company of these women and overjoyed she was able to address many of them by name. Who would have thought when she left San Francisco a few days ago she would end up here? Not alone or surrounded by strangers, but among friends.

Her assignment no longer felt like a job. It felt like coming home.

And then there was Luisa. Finn glanced at the picture Luisa had taken of her and Porky Pig in the airport bar in Dallas. Then she slid over to the photograph she had taken of Luisa at the hotel less than a mile away. Luisa was smiling and happy in the photo, her brown skin standing in sharp contrast to the white sheets tangled around her semi-covered body.

Finn hadn't felt the need to define their relationship then, but she needed some boundaries now. Was Luisa a friend? Was she a lover? Or was she something else entirely?

Finn had never felt this way before. This strange combination of falling and flying she experienced each time she heard Luisa's voice or called her image to mind. Was this what it felt like to be in love, or was Montezuma exacting an entirely different kind of revenge?

The only time she had felt something remotely similar was back in high school when she realized she couldn't mend Nancy Everhart's broken heart because she wanted to be the one Nancy was crying over instead of the quarterback who had dumped her for the head cheerleader. Then she had attributed the feeling to finding herself. Now it was due to finding someone else.

She had been searching for something her whole life. A new destination, a new experience. Always something new. And always just out of reach. Was Luisa who she had been searching for this whole time? Could Luisa give her everything she had been trying to find, or would she keep waiting for the phone to ring? For the next adventure to come calling. Could she stop trying to outrun the past and enjoy the present?

Finn powered off her camera and looked back to see

how far she had walked during the thirty minutes since she had left the resort. The Mariposa was still in sight but several properties away. Dozens more multimillion-dollar hotels and resorts loomed in the distance. She looped her camera strap over her shoulder and kept going, though the hotels on the end of the beach seemed just as far away as they had when she'd first set out on her spur-of-the-moment journey.

After another hour of walking, she resigned herself to the fact she wouldn't make it to the end of the spit of land curling in the distance. On foot, the trip would probably take at least two hours one way, and Mother Nature had other plans. Finn watched as dark clouds began to roll in, obscuring the hotels on the far end of the beach and sending frustrated sunbathers in search of shelter. Then she moved out of the way as the twelve camouflage-clad Federal Police patrolling the area drove their four all-terrain vehicles toward Mariposa's end of the beach.

"Do you need a lift, miss?" one driver asked after he skidded to a stop.

"No, thanks. I'm fine."

The two gunmen on the back of the ATV eyed her up and down before the roar of a passing speedboat forced them to turn their attention back to the water, where several windsurfers and two parasailers were continuing to play despite the bad weather slowly making its way toward them.

Finn felt a sudden sense of foreboding but attributed it to the dark skies in the distance and the ominous roll of thunder that made the sand vibrate beneath her bare feet. The storm was closing in fast.

"You've got about thirty minutes before the skies open up," the driver said. "I suggest you head for cover if you don't want to get wet." He flashed a disarming grin. "Don't you hate it when it rains in paradise?"

He flipped his visor over his eyes and sped off without waiting for an answer. The gunmen kept one arm curled around their assault rifles and wrapped the other around the rollover bar that had been attached to the modified vehicle.

Finn squinted as the ATV's oversized wheels kicked up sand in its wake. The encounter with the policemen reminded her of Luisa. Luisa had the same professional manner the driver had shown, and Finn bet she'd look great in camouflage. Great. Even more fuel for her fantasies.

Not for the first time, Finn wondered when—or if—she and Luisa would see each other again. Had their encounter in Dallas been the only one they would have, or would it turn out to be the first of many?

Luisa wasn't the first woman Finn had met while she was on the road, but Luisa was definitely the first she longed to see again. And the first she was reluctant to leave. But how could she possibly stay when leaving was what she did best? For her, saying good-bye was infinitely easier than saying hello. Or sometimes saying anything at all.

She headed to the bar as the first drops of rain began to fall. She ordered a drink as the room started to fill. When her phone rang, she was surprised to see it was Luisa calling several hours before she expected to hear from her.

"I would ask how things were going," Luisa said, "but from the sound of it, I'd say things were going quite well."

Finn tipped the bartender a dollar for her mojito and moved to a quieter locale so she could hear better. She slipped inside the theater, where several women were auditioning for Lovers and Friends, the game that would provide tomorrow night's entertainment. The competition was an SOS favorite and pitted two sets of best friends against two couples to see who knew more about the other, those who were in a platonic relationship or those who were in a romantic one. Finn had read that some women couldn't wait to enter the competition while others would rather watch others squirm than put their own relationships on the line by not being able to provide the right answers to questions such as her pet name for her lover's lady parts or the most unusual place they'd had sex.

Finn saw Jill and Ryan in the crowd of hopefuls. Communication appeared to be the key to doing well in the game, but Jill and Ryan seemed to have a distinct lack of it, considering Jill was in love with Ryan and Ryan didn't seem to realize it. Nevertheless, she gave them a thumbs-up to show her support for their quest to be chosen over the dozens of applicants.

"This is new," Finn said, keeping her voice low so she wouldn't disturb the auditions.

"I was following up on some leads on a cold case. My appointment ended earlier than I expected, so I decided to check in with you before I headed back to the office."

"Did you catch the bad guys?"

"Not yet. I spent the afternoon beating my head against a wall of silence, but I feel like I may be on to something. I'll know more tomorrow."

Finn noticed Luisa answered the question without providing any details about where she had been or who she had gone to see. Not that Finn wanted to know. She hated the idea of Luisa risking her life over what was probably a lost cause—ending Mexico's drug trade was an impossible task hundreds of other law enforcement officials had tried and failed to accomplish—but she admired Luisa's persistence.

"But I didn't call to talk shop," Luisa said. "I called to let you know I have a dinner date Saturday night."

Finn felt a pang of jealousy until she heard the mirth in Luisa's voice. "So you and Javier are finally going to get together?"

"Mrs. Villalobos offered me *tamales*. How could I say no?"

"So food is the way to your heart. I've been going about this the wrong way. I thought all I needed to do was to ply you with beer and ironic humor."

"That's how you get me in bed, but it isn't how you get me to stay."

"No? How do I do that?" Finn held her breath, anxious to hear Luisa's response.

"I could tell you, but that would be taking the easy way out. You strike me as someone who would rather discover things on her own than be spoon-fed the answer. That's you in a nutshell, isn't it?"

Finn laughed softly, remembering the way Luisa's face lit up when she was amused and how it glowed when she made love. How could someone who could be so warm and loving in bed be made of steel at work? Was it the gun, the badge, or something inside her that helped her make the change? Finn didn't know the answer, but she looked forward to finding it.

"How do you know so much about me, super cop?"

"I can tell everything I need to know about a woman by the way she makes love."

Finn scooted down in her seat. She wished she had taken Luisa's call in her room instead of a public place. Then she could have been free to steer the conversation in a much different direction.

"Is that what that was back in Dallas, an interrogation technique? If so, you are *really* good at your job. Perhaps I should plead the Fifth next time."

"That wouldn't be nearly as much fun, though, would it?" Luisa's voice deepened the way it had in the bar. When she had invited Finn to follow her and Finn had done so without thinking twice. "But I'm sure I could still find a way to make you talk."

"I'd like to see you try."

"Is that a dare?"

"I would never dare someone who's licensed to carry a gun. Consider it a challenge instead."

"In that case, challenge accepted."

Finn shuddered, her body awash in memories—and a fresh wave of desire. She wondered how upset Brett would be if she blew off tomorrow afternoon's activities in favor of a day trip to Mexico City. She and Luisa had crammed a lifetime into two hours. Imagine what they could do with four or more. Unfortunately, this time the risk exceeded the reward. Luisa had to work, and if she didn't complete her assignment, Brett might conveniently lose her number when it was time for a new one. Then where would she be? Miserable and missing a paycheck, that's where.

"By the time I'm done," Luisa said, "you're going to tell me everything there is to know about you."

Finn usually liked leaving some things unsaid to provide an air of mystery, but Luisa made her want to open up and spill all her secrets. She wanted to share herself with Luisa. In every way. But if she put herself out there, she didn't want to do it alone.

"Do you promise to return the favor?" she asked.

"Of course. What do you want to know first?"

"Everything."

"That could take a while."

"That's what I'm counting on. So when you call me tonight, start from the beginning and go slow."

"Whatever you say, *mariposa*."

"See how much easier life is when you agree with me?"

"I see how much easier my life is with you in it. That means something, doesn't it?"

Finn's breath caught. This was the point when she usually ran the other way. Fighting her instincts, she decided to move closer.

"It means everything."

❖

Luisa didn't like to bring her work home with her, but she couldn't stop thinking about the trip she had made to Santa Martha Jail that afternoon. She wanted to forget the jeers and whistles that had greeted her arrival. She wanted to forget the smell of piss, shit, and sweat that assaulted her nose. She wanted to forget the fruitless interview she had conducted with Salvador Perez, a sullen teenager too caught up in the vicious cycle of machismo, fear, and intimidation to answer her questions. And most of all, she wanted to forget Director Chavez ripping her a new asshole for planning to visit Perez's mother in Agua Dulce tomorrow without taking backup along for the ride. He had praised her dedication and investigative instincts just as he had during their first meeting, but that had come long after he had started his harangue.

"Haven't we already had this conversation? I need you to be a team player, Moreno, not a free agent," he had said, conveniently forgetting he was partially responsible for isolating her from everyone else. He had chained her to a desk until she could earn her coworkers' respect instead of their enmity. But how was she supposed to do her job when she had more shackles on her than most prisoners?

"Fine," she had said. "I'll take Ruben Huerta."

"Huerta? That beanpole from Records? He couldn't catch a cold, let alone a hardened criminal."

"Ruben has a vested interest in helping me crack this case. Carlos Ramos was his friend. I trust him, sir. I know he'll have my back."

Director Chavez had eyed her for a long moment, obviously debating whether to accept her suggestion, tell her to take someone else, or advise her to use the government's precious resources on a fresher case.

"What are you hoping to accomplish tomorrow?" he had finally asked.

"At the very least, I want to identify the four men in those pictures and help bring some closure to the family members still wondering where they are and what happened to them. And if I can tie them to the Jaguars, it could bring us a step closer to identifying the leaders of the organization."

Director Chavez had closed Perez's case file and pushed it across the desk. "Then go. Just make sure you and Huerta come back in one piece."

Luisa packed a bag and placed it by her apartment door. Agua Dulce was a good eight hours away—more if the dirt roads surrounding it had been washed out by the spring rains—and she wanted to get an early start. After she conducted her interview, she and Ruben would stay in Agua Dulce overnight and head back to Mexico City on Thursday. She had barely set the bag down when someone knocked on her door.

"Going somewhere?"

As Mrs. Villalobos eyed the rucksack, Luisa was glad she had tucked Salvador Perez's case file inside the bag instead of leaving it on top. Luisa thought the woman was harmless, but she was too curious for her own good. Not to mention she loved to talk. If she said something to the wrong person, Luisa's investigation could end before it had barely begun.

"I'm taking a day trip tomorrow."

"Somewhere nice, I hope."

"It's for work, so I don't know how nice it will be."

"Ooh. That sounds exciting." Mrs. Villalobos invited herself in and took a look around the apartment. "Nice and neat. Everything in its place. You're a definite improvement over the young man who lived here before you moved in. He was a police officer, too. Ramos, I think his name was. Carlos Ramos. Yes, that's it. He was nice enough, but I have to say he was a bit of a slob. I'm not surprised. He kept a lot of late hours so he didn't have time to clean or have a decent meal. I think he lived on cigarettes and coffee."

"Why did he move out?" Luisa asked, trying to hide her surprise that Carlos Ramos had once lived in the apartment she currently occupied.

Mrs. Villalobos shrugged. "I woke up one morning and he was gone. Everyone in the building knew he had money problems. I think he was behind on his rent. He probably left before he could be evicted. I heard he's been reported missing, but I think he's on the lam from all the bill collectors he owed money. Unless they got to him and taught him a lesson for not being able to pay. Never buy what you can't afford. That's always been my motto."

"Is there anything that goes on in this neighborhood you don't know?" Luisa could picture Mrs. Villalobos holding vigil in front of her apartment window, binoculars at the ready.

"Someone has to keep an eye on things. It might as well be me."

"What brings you to see me?" Luisa was enjoying the pleasant diversion Mrs. Villalobos's presence offered, but she was planning to make it an early night and she had a call to make before she turned in for the evening.

"I was curious about something." Mrs. Villalobos reached into the folds of her housedress and pulled out a postcard. "The postman delivered this to me by mistake. I was wondering."

She turned the card over, flipping from the picturesque scene on the front to the handwritten words on the back. "Who's Finn?"

Luisa plucked the card from Mrs. Villalobos's hands before her nosy neighbor could read any more of the words she'd probably already memorized.

"A friend from up north."

"A close friend?"

Luisa felt a blush creep up the back of her neck. "We're still working that part out."

Mrs. Villalobos flashed a knowing smile. "I'll tell Javier not to get his hopes up about Saturday night. Seeing as how you might already be spoken for. What does Finn do? He must make good money if he's staying at the Mariposa. The rooms there cost four hundred dollars a night."

"She's a writer."

Luisa waited for the familiar look of disapproval she received when she revealed her sexual orientation to someone of Mrs. Villalobos's generation, a group set in their ways and who placed inordinate value on the traditional roles for men and women she had no desire to fulfill.

Mrs. Villalobos's eyes twinkled, making her look much younger than her years. For a moment, Luisa saw the vibrant young woman she used to be instead of the more mature one she was now.

"There's room for everyone, I always say. Even…writers."

"I'll be sure to tell Finn you said that."

"Give her my best the next time you speak to her. Even though I can't count on you becoming my granddaughter-in-law anymore, are we still on for dinner Saturday night?"

"I wouldn't miss it for the world."

Luisa gave Mrs. Villalobos a hug, then showed her to the door. When she was alone, she turned her attention to the postcard Finn had sent her. Mariposa Resort and Spa was printed on the front, along with a picture of a bikini-clad woman staring wistfully at the sun setting over the Caribbean. The back read, "Thinking of you. Wish you were here—Finn."

Luisa propped the postcard against the stack of unread books on her coffee table and reached for her cell phone. Finn answered on the third ring. As usual, there was a riot of noise in the background. This time, it sounded like there was a concert going on. Luisa heard the bluesy vocal stylings of a raspy-voiced woman who sounded like the love child of Janis Joplin and Melissa Etheridge.

"Is that Sarah Burress?" she asked.

"Yep. Sure is."

"I watched her compete on the American version of *Singing Star*. The guy she lost to was good, but Sarah was ten times better. Too bad the voters threw their support behind the boy band reject instead of the lesbian with a shaved head."

"Hold on. Let me put you on speaker."

Finn held up her phone so Luisa could listen to a few bars.

"Now I wish I was there, too."

"You got my card."

"Actually, Mrs. Villalobos got your card, but she was nice enough to share it with me. She says hi, by the way. And she wanted me to let you know she doesn't hold the fact that you're a writer against you. My ex-future husband's comments were less than favorable, I'm sure."

"I'm so sorry to hear that," Finn said, though she sounded anything but.

"Tell me why someone who is as smart and funny as you isn't in a relationship."

"I don't do relationships."

"Why not?"

"I-I'm never home," Finn said after a brief hesitation.

"That sounds more like an excuse than a legitimate reason."

"Maybe I'm not as perfect as you think I am. Maybe I'm not the glamorous world traveler I appear to be but an introvert with communication issues."

"Maybe I like introverts with communication issues. The introverts I know always feel like they're expected to apologize for who they are instead of saying, 'This is me. Take it or leave it.' Is that how you feel?"

"Yes, it is." A wistful note had seeped into Finn's voice. She seemed to be about to say something else. To reveal something deeply personal. Luisa prepared herself to hear Finn's confession. Then the moment passed. "Enough about me. What's your excuse? Why are you still single?"

Luisa wanted to say, "Because I hadn't met you yet," but she guessed it would make Finn turn tail and run. Finn already seemed to have her eye on the door half the time. Luisa didn't want to help push her through it.

"Like you, I don't want to commit to anyone unless I know I'm going to be there for her day in and day out. If I wash out at this job, the only thing I want to leave behind is an empty apartment."

"And what kind of woman can you see yourself with when you're finally ready to settle down?"

"Someone who makes me laugh and isn't afraid to laugh at herself. Someone who likes adventure but is equally content spending a quiet evening at home. Someone who's independent but knows when to ask for help."

Finn sighed. "She sounds perfect. I want to meet someone like that, too."

You are that person, mariposa. *You just don't know it yet.*

"If you don't hear from me tomorrow, I'm not ignoring you," she said. "I have to make a road trip, and most small towns here don't have the best cell phone signals."

"Should I be worried?"

Luisa knew better than to tell Finn her concerns were misplaced because Finn was savvy enough to see through the lie.

"I'll be careful."

"You'd better. Who else is going to find my stories as fascinating as you do?"

Luisa wished it was only Finn's stories she found fascinating. Because if she wasn't careful, when Finn packed her bags and flew back to America on Saturday, she was going to take Luisa's heart with her.

Day Five

Finn tapped her foot in time with the music as she waited in line for a barbecue lunch on the beach. It felt incongruous to be listening to a reggae band playing a medley of Bob Marley's hits in a country where the primary language was Spanish, but Cancún was located on the Caribbean, so she supposed it made sense. Nothing else in her life seemed to, though.

She didn't feel like herself. She wasn't acting like herself. She didn't talk about her past, yet she had come close to telling Luisa all about it last night. She hadn't said anything because it hadn't felt like the right time, but the urge to confide in Luisa was still there. The familiar urge to flee had gone missing, however. So had her ever-present itch for something new. At the moment, the only things she craved were the steaks the chef was pulling off the charcoal grill and Luisa's kiss. The former she would have in a matter of minutes. The latter would have to wait. Perhaps forever.

She tried not to think about what Luisa might be up to today, but her mind kept forcing her to consider the possibility Luisa might not make it back.

When she had asked Luisa on the phone last night if she needed to be worried, Luisa hadn't responded with the reassuring "no" she needed to hear, but a more measured "I'll be careful." The difference could be a matter of life and death. Luisa's.

Of course Luisa would take all the necessary precautions. That was what she had been trained to do. But what about the other guy? If the person Luisa planned to talk to didn't like something she said, would the visit end in flying fists or bullets? One was much easier to avoid than the other. And far less deadly.

The uncertainty gave Finn chills despite the warm breeze blowing across her skin. Her anxiety continued to grow as the hours slowly crawled by with no word from Luisa. She nearly jumped a mile when someone behind her in line goosed her in the back.

"I didn't mean to scare you." Ryan held up her hands in mock surrender. "I just wanted to know if you'd mind if I hang out with you during the trip to Chichén Itzá tomorrow. Jill and I signed up a few days ago, but she's backing out because she heard the resort's having a *lucha libre* exhibition tomorrow instead of the presentation on Aztec culture they had originally planned."

"That's a drastic change. Why the switch?"

"The lecturer got sick and had to cancel," Jill said.

"Now she's geeking out like a fangirl at a Xena convention and she's sending me off to Chicken Pizza by myself," Ryan said.

"Have you seen those guys?" Jill asked. "Some of them may be a little soft in the middle, but they're all incredible athletes. They put on an even better show than the wrestlers in WWE. At home, I love watching them fly around the ring on TV. Now I get to do it in person. I can't miss an opportunity like that."

"You're choosing guys in masks and spandex tights over

one of the Seven Wonders of the modern world? Nice move, fangirl." Ryan turned back to Finn. "If the guide makes us partner up for some reason, will you be mine?" Her gray eyes displayed a vulnerability her muscle-bound body and outgoing personality had previously been able to hide.

Even the life of the party gets lonely sometimes, too. Good to know.

"Sure." Finn loaded her paper plate with a roll, an assortment of fresh fruit, and a mixed green salad to serve as side dishes to the slices of sizzling sirloin she had received from the sweat-drenched chef manning the grill. "I'll be glad to hold your hand and help you cross the street."

"You've been hanging around this one too long." Ryan jerked her thumb toward Jill while she dug a teasing elbow into Finn's ribs. "But, thanks. I owe you one. Tomorrow night, your first drink is on me."

Jill rolled her eyes. "It's amazing how easy free drinks are to come by when they're all-inclusive."

"In that case," Finn said, reaching for a cup of sangria, "I'll take two."

And when the time came, she hoped she'd be raising her glass in honor of a fun-filled day, not in Luisa's memory.

❖

The drive to Agua Dulce took closer to ten hours than eight, the last two spent on roads so badly rutted Luisa feared the rental car's suspension would never be the same again. When she and Ruben finally arrived at a maze of densely crowded shacks and "houses" constructed of cinder blocks, tar paper, and sheets of rust-covered corrugated tin, she got out of the car and stretched her numb legs and aching back.

Then she clipped her badge to the waistband of her black slacks and pulled on her blazer to cover the gun holstered high on her left side.

Ruben climbed out the passenger's side of the car and slammed the door behind him.

"Which house do you think belongs to Silvia Perez?"

Luisa slipped her sunglasses into her jacket's inside pocket and peered at the dozens of wary faces staring back at her.

"It's supposed to be 1632," she said, referring to the case file. "But good luck figuring out which one that is."

Some of the houses didn't have doors or windows. Others barely had walls. Splurging on house numbers was out of the question.

"What are we supposed to do?"

"Ask someone."

Beads of moisture formed on Ruben's upper lip as sweat dampened his white dress shirt.

"Relax," Luisa said. "We're the good guys, remember?"

"I think someone forgot to tell them that."

All around them, villagers began retreating into their homes or making themselves look busy.

"I'm looking for Silvia Perez. Also known as Silvia Quintanilla," Luisa said to a short woman balancing an overflowing laundry basket on her head. "Do you know where I can find her?"

"I don't know anything," the woman said as she rushed past them and made her way to the river.

Agua Dulce meant "sweet water" in Spanish, but the brown body of water that served as the villagers' Laundromat, bathtub, and toilet looked decidedly sour.

Luisa and Ruben approached several more people, but were met with the same stubborn refusals each time. After twenty minutes of wandering through the village with nothing to show for it, Ruben pulled a handkerchief from his pocket, cleaned the condensation on his glasses, then dried his sweat-soaked face.

"How did a kid from a place like this end up working for the most powerful cartel in the country?"

Luisa took another look at the soul-crushing poverty surrounding them. "If you were forced to live like this, wouldn't you do anything you could to get out, too?"

Ruben scraped his shoes against the back of a scraggly jacaranda tree to clean the mud caked on the soles. "I see your point."

"Heads up. We have company."

Luisa reached for her gun when she saw five men in a battered pickup truck slowly approach. Two were sitting in the cab and three were standing in the truck bed. The three in the back were armed with rifles so old they might have been used in the Revolution. The oldest of the five men, a weather-beaten man somewhere between fifty and seventy, slid out of the driver's seat.

"Are you from the Federal Police?" he asked after spitting a dark brown stream of tobacco juice on the ground.

Luisa let her hand drop when she realized the men were what passed for law around here. "We are."

"Then where were you last night when we needed you?"

Luisa shared a look with Ruben, who appeared to be as confused as she was.

"I don't understand."

"The people in this village are too scared to talk to you, but I'm not." The man removed his sweat-stained cowboy hat and used it to fan his face. "My name is Miguel Serrano. If you're looking for Silvia Perez, follow me."

"What should we do?" Ruben asked as Miguel headed back to his truck.

Luisa climbed into the rental car.

"We follow the man."

Miguel didn't lead them far. He parked his truck on a hill overlooking the river. A series of crude, handmade crosses marked the land as a cemetery.

"Over there," he said, pointing to a row of shrouded bodies lying next to six freshly dug graves.

Luisa squatted and carefully pulled one of the sheets aside, revealing the bullet-riddled body of a man who had probably been handsome once upon a time but was now grossly disfigured by the damage that had been inflicted before and after his gruesome death. In addition to gunshot wounds to his eyes, cheek, chest, and the back of his head, there were stab wounds to his stomach, cigarette burns on his arms, and contusions on his face.

"Antonio Perez. He was Silvia's husband and Salvador Perez's father," Miguel said. "That's Silvia next to him. The other bodies belong to their children. The youngest was only four."

"What's this bruising around their mouths?"

Luisa used the beam of her penlight to point out the discolored flesh on each victim's battered face.

"Their tongues were cut out as a sign of what happens to people who talk to the police."

Ruben stumbled a few feet away, bent over double, and vomited up the greasy quesadillas they had eaten for lunch. Struggling to concentrate over the sound of Ruben's retching, Luisa took several photos of the bodies, then pulled out her notebook.

"What happened?" she asked.

"First things first."

Miguel motioned for his men to take care of the corpses. After the bodies were lowered into the ground, Miguel said a few words over them. Then his men picked up shovels and began filling in the graves.

"Hit men raided the village last night," Miguel said. "They knew exactly what they were looking for because they were in and out before my men and I arrived."

"That kind of damage takes time to inflict. Were there any witnesses?"

"Plenty. But—"

Luisa finished his sentence for him.

"They're too scared to talk." She glanced at the tiny village inhabited by frightened people forced to turn a blind eye to the atrocities they had observed in order to save their own lives. Then she turned back to Miguel. "Do you think the hit men were working for the Jaguars, the Sinaloa cartel, or the Zs?"

Miguel spat out another stream of tobacco.

"Pardon my language, but the fucking Jaguars, of course. Who else could go into and out of a crowded village without leaving a trace?"

"No one." Ruben wiped his mouth with the back of his hand. "And whoever did this didn't either. Not with all this mud around." He pointed to the road leading to the heart of Agua Dulce. "I'll bet not much traffic goes through here. We need to take impressions of the freshest tire tracks. The ones that don't match our car or your truck have to belong to the vehicle or vehicles the hit men drove last night. Once Officer Moreno and I get back to headquarters, we can scan the images to try to match the tires to the ones used by the make and model of a car that might have been seen in the area."

Luisa slapped him on the shoulder.

"I knew there was a reason I brought you along. Miguel, where's the nearest place we can find the supplies we need to make the molds?"

"I've got chicken wire, wood, and a bag of concrete mix in my truck. My farm's not too far from here. I was planning to repair the fence surrounding my cow pasture after I finished up here, but the supplies are yours if you can use them."

"You're a lifesaver."

"No," he said, casting a forlorn look at the six new graves in the small cemetery. "I'm just a man."

Luisa felt unpardonable guilt.

"Did this happen because of me? Did that family die because I asked the wrong questions?"

"No, young lady." Miguel placed a callused hand on her arm. "They died because you asked the right ones."

One day, Luisa hoped, she would get the right answers.

She, Ruben, Miguel, and his men walked back to the village so their vehicles wouldn't obscure the tire tracks any more than they had already.

"Who knew we were coming?" Ruben asked as two of Miguel's men stirred water from the river into a pot filled with concrete mix.

Luisa carefully considered the question before answering. "No one except you, me, and Director Chavez."

"I doubt the director would betray his own people. Perhaps someone saw you talking to Salvador Perez at the jail and assumed—correctly, as it turns out—you would head here next."

"You're probably right, but dozens of people saw me enter the jail and meet with Salvador. Any of them could be the potential snitch. Anyone from the inmates to the guards to the warden."

Her frustration was mounting by the minute. Every time she thought she was taking a step forward, she ended up getting pushed back two.

Ruben poured concrete into the first set of tracks and

waited for it to set. When it was dry, he carefully placed it into a makeshift mold.

"Exhibit number one."

Luisa placed a numbered tag in front of the mold and photographed it from several angles. Then she and Ruben repeated the process on the rest of the tracks.

"We can't stay here tonight," Ruben said when they were done. "It isn't safe."

"I know."

Luisa had planned to rent a hotel room somewhere between here and home and drive back to Mexico City in the morning, but those plans had changed. The hit men were probably long gone, but if they were still in the area, they could ambush her and Ruben on the road, or follow them to the hotel and attack them in their sleep as they'd done with the Perez family here in Agua Dulce. She looked around, wondering if she and Ruben were being watched right now.

"How do I tell Salvador Perez his entire family's been killed?"

"Word travels fast in the prison system," Ruben said. "I have a feeling he already knows. He might even be next on the chopping block."

Luisa checked her phone but, as expected, she didn't have a signal. She and Ruben were on their own.

"I'll call the warden at Santa Martha during the drive back and ask for Perez to be placed in protective custody until I can interview him again," she said. "If this doesn't convince him to tell me what he knows, nothing will."

"Sounds good to me. Now let's get the hell out of here."

As Ruben buckled himself into the passenger's seat of the rental car, Luisa tossed her jacket in the backseat, slid behind the wheel, and began the long drive back to Mexico City.

Ruben tuned the radio to a station playing a *narcocorrido*, a mournful ode to a former drug lord whose violent life and gruesome death had made him a macabre folk hero in some circles. The subject of the song wasn't the only narco whose exploits had been set to music. Joaquín "El Chapo" Guzman's second escape from federal prison had practically inspired an entire cottage industry. Luisa flipped to something less depressing.

It was days like today that made her question her chosen profession. She felt like a dog chasing its tail. Were the danger, loneliness, and self-imposed isolation worth the hours of wasted effort? Today it certainly didn't feel like it.

She could be making love to Finn in Cancún right now instead of driving across the countryside with one eye on the road and the other in her rearview mirror as she tried to make sure she and Ruben weren't being followed by someone who had been ordered to track them down and kill them.

Perhaps her parents were right. Perhaps she should find something else to do for a living and leave this seemingly impossible mission to someone else.

No, she told herself as she left Agua Dulce and its unspeakable carnage behind. She had joined the army because she wanted to fight for her country. She had become a member of the Federal Police for the same reason. She couldn't give up now just because she had run into a few roadblocks. She had to keep fighting. For herself, for her people, and for Finn.

She felt herself falling for Finn a little more each day, but she refused to put Finn's life at risk by drawing her deeper into hers. She couldn't—wouldn't—allow herself to even consider the possibility of being with Finn until she had done her part to make Mexico the idyllic place the tourist offices advertised instead of the war zone it could occasionally turn out to be.

Despite today's setback, she needed to complete her quest. Her life—and her future—depended on it.

Day Six

Finn shoved her camera, a bottle of sunscreen, a baseball cap, her e-reader, and a bottle of water into her backpack. The literature Veronique, the clerk in the excursions office, had given her suggested she should bring a light jacket for the return trip, but she expected to be so hot and sweaty from spending two hours walking in the heat and humidity of the Mexican jungle she would welcome the chill of the air-conditioning on the tour company's chartered bus.

She slipped her cell phone into the pocket of her cargo shorts, looked around her room for anything she might have forgotten, and headed to the main restaurant for breakfast.

The trepidation she had felt yesterday had evaporated after she read the text Luisa sent her at nearly four a.m. *Finally home. Exhausted. Have fun in Chichén Itzá. I'll call you tonight so you can tell me all about it. I can't wait to hear about your latest adventure.* And Finn couldn't wait to live it. Now that she knew Luisa had made it home safe and sound, she could relax and enjoy whatever the day had in store.

She walked—okay, floated—down the two flights of stairs and headed for the flower-lined walkway next to the sea. She hadn't seen the grounds this deserted in days. It was so early even the iguanas weren't up yet. The white-clad security guards were already at their posts, however. She nodded good morning to one speaking rapid Spanish into a walkie-talkie. His spiked hair and tattooed arms gave him a rough edge that contrasted with the more sedate appearance of the clean-cut guards she had seen stationed near the beach over the past week. Those guys looked like they could double as Secret Service agents. This guy looked more like a bouncer in a biker bar.

As she neared the heart of the resort, she passed a trio of maids in coral-colored uniforms reporting to work. Their *holas* were more subdued than normal, but she attributed that to running into them before they'd had their morning coffee. And vice versa. She normally didn't start feeling human on most mornings until she'd had her second cup of joe. Today she was still waiting to have her first. When she reached the restaurant, nearly thirty women were gathered at the foot of the winding stairs, and more were on the way.

"Grab a seat," Ryan said, straddling one of the stone benches outside the gift shop. "They're not open yet."

Finn checked her watch. Six forty. The restaurant's doors were supposed to be open ten minutes ago to give everyone plenty of time to have a hearty breakfast before they left for their respective excursions. So much for two cups of coffee. Today she would have to settle for one. If that.

"What's the holdup?" she asked. The bus was leaving in less than an hour, and she needed to fuel up before she boarded. The granola bar, apple, and banana in her backpack were supposed to be a snack. They weren't supposed to last all day. "The resort employees aren't on strike again, are they?"

If so, that could explain the new security guard she had seen, along with the maids' dour mood.

"That would be perfect, wouldn't it? Maybe the chef forgot to set his alarm clock." Ryan laid her head on her folded arms to catch twenty winks while she waited, but she perked up as soon as a pretty blonde wearing an Indie necklace sat next to her. "Are you headed to Chichén Itzá, too?"

"No, I'm going ziplining in Tulum."

"That sounds fun." Ryan winked in Finn's direction. "I wonder if it's too late for me to change my reservation."

"After the hard time you gave Jill about backing out to watch wrestling, yeah, I think it is."

"You're probably right. She'd never let me live it down if I did."

Finn sat across from her. "How long have you two been friends?"

"Practically since we came out of the womb. My earliest and best memories all have her in them."

"Then why aren't you together?"

Ryan shrugged. "I've thought about it. She's the coolest woman I've ever met. And she must have the patience of Job if she puts up with my shit and keeps coming back for more."

"But?"

"I'm horrible at relationships, and I don't want to risk losing my best friend if I screw things up."

Finn hadn't known Luisa as long as Ryan and Jill had known each other, but she could apply the same reasoning to their relationship. What she had with Luisa was exciting and fun. It gave her something to look forward to at the end of each day. But what would happen if they tried to take their relationship to the next level? Would their feelings deepen like the flavors in a long-simmering stew or crumble under the weight of expectation like a flattened soufflé? Finn had always preferred to keep things light, but she was starting to develop a taste for something heartier.

A cheer went up when the restaurant's doors finally opened. As the harried-looking wait staff tried to deal with the influx of hungry diners, Finn filled her plate with plenty of protein and grabbed more fruit from the salad bar in case her current stash ran out before they returned to the resort in time for a late lunch. She and Ryan shared a table with a couple of retired history teachers from Ohio. Finn assumed the teachers were going to Chichén Itzá, too, but they said they were planning to catch a cab and head into town on their own for a day of retail therapy.

"I'm starting to think Jill wasn't the only one who bailed on us today," Ryan said after breakfast as she and Finn walked to the front of the hotel to check in with their tour bus.

"You might want to retract that statement." Finn took a long look at the eager faces peering out the bus's tinted windows. "It appears we still have a full crew."

"Cool. I didn't want us to be the only ones getting a liberal dose of culture today."

Ryan was easy on the eyes and effortlessly charming. Finn could see why Jill had fallen for her, but she preferred a certain Federal Police officer currently residing in Mexico City. Luisa was easy on the eyes, too. And her adorable peach pit dimples were absolutely to die for.

Poor choice of words.

She found a seat near the back of the bus and claimed the spot by the window so she could watch the scenery roll by. The driver closed the doors promptly at seven thirty and pulled out of the parking lot.

"Wake me when this part is over."

Ryan scrunched down in her seat, folded her arms across her chest, and closed her eyes as the guide, Richard Haarhuis, introduced himself and began a lecture on the ancient Mayans' many contributions to the modern world.

Finn felt her own eyelids grow heavy during Richard's discourse on the Mayans' counting system, a precursor of the binary code used by computer programmers. She perked up when the driver left the highly commercialized areas of Cancún behind and headed toward the parts of the city the jungle seemed intent on reclaiming.

Ramshackle houses and huts dotted the landscape, some structures not much more than tarp-covered lean-tos constructed to protect their occupants from the blazing sun. Elaborate ads for soft drinks and high-end electronics adorned commercial buildings, while crude hand-painted signs for various political candidates had been affixed to houses or staked in tiny front yards.

Finn snapped pictures of Mr. Carnitas, a downscale-looking restaurant with an upscale-sounding name. Then she captured a field of towering agave plants that would one day provide the essence of hundreds of bottles of tequila. Finally, she found herself gazing upon a well-tended cemetery next to what could only be called a shantytown.

"Even in the poorest neighborhoods," Richard said, "people make sure their relatives' final resting places are cared for. In Mexico, death is treated as a cause for celebration, not mourning. If you come back this way on Saturday or Sunday, you might see groups of families having a picnic lunch with the people who have passed on."

Finn lowered her camera out of respect. This was the part of the country she wasn't supposed to see. Which was the real Mexico? The ritzy hotels lining the beach, or the flimsy houses that looked like they would fall over the next time a strong wind blew through?

"We're going to stop at the flea market up here on the left," Richard announced halfway to Chichén Itzá. "It has clean restrooms, and it offers you a place to walk around and stretch your legs. You can buy souvenirs if you want, but be warned it's the same stuff you can get anywhere else. The bus leaves in fifteen minutes. Please be on time. I don't want to leave without you, but I will if you're late. Then you'll have to find your own way back to the hotel. From here, a cab ride should be about a hundred bucks. Your choice."

Ryan had woken up from her nap somewhere between the agave field and the cemetery.

"I like this guy," she said. "He's not full of BS like the guides who make side deals with all the vendors lining the route and try to talk you into buying a bunch of crap you don't need."

"Veronique said he was one of the best."

"What was it he said about getting your name or a special date turned into a Mayan hieroglyph?"

"If you write it down now and give it to the vendors at the gate when we arrive, the finished product will be ready by the time we complete the tour."

"I think I'll get them to do the day Jill and I met. That way, she could feel like she was part of this trip even though she didn't take part. Do you think she'd like that?"

"I think she'd love it."

Finn thought about making a similar gesture for Luisa but decided against it. Luisa had already been to Chichén Itzá and probably had a boxful of souvenirs to commemorate the trip. If Finn bought her a souvenir, it had to be something Luisa didn't already have. It had to be something special. Something unique. Something like the Porky Pig toy Finn had given her before they parted ways last week. Saturday once seemed so far away. Now it was much too close.

She wondered if her relationship with Luisa could continue in some way despite her upcoming change in locale. They had distance between them now. A few more miles couldn't make that much of a difference, could they? Besides, her phone worked just as well in San Francisco as it did in

Cancún. Maybe this time—for the first time—writing "the end" at the bottom of a story could mean a beginning instead of a conclusion.

She shuffled toward the front of the bus and climbed down the stairs. Outside, she took pictures of the primitive drawings of the Chichén Itzá pyramids painted on the weathered metal sign on the sprawling building's roof and of the handwoven blankets hanging in an artisan's display area. Then she joined the bathroom line, where Ryan was taking five-dollar bets on who would be last to board the bus.

"My money's on the Barbies," she said, referring to the femme couple with teased hair and matching outfits who hadn't checked in for the trip until a few minutes before the driver closed the doors. "They look like serious shopaholics."

"I'll take that bet."

Ryan grudgingly paid up after the Barbies were the first to leave the tchotchke-laden confines of the flea market and Finn's pick, a pair of school bus drivers from San Diego, were the last. "How did you know?"

"If I've learned anything from this trip," Finn said, pocketing the money, "it's that people aren't always what they seem."

❖

Luisa expected Mrs. Villalobos to be waiting for her when she exited her apartment. As usual, she wasn't disappointed. Mrs. Villalobos took a long look at her and frowned in disapproval.

"You look tired. Did you have a long night?"

"Short night, long day."

Luisa had fallen into bed shortly after texting Finn and had slept hard until her alarm went off five hours later.

Director Chavez had told her she could take the day off when she called him on the road from Agua Dulce, but she didn't want her investigation to lose any of the momentum it might have gained yesterday. The case of the four unidentified men had been cold for years, but it was starting to heat up. She needed to act before the trail cooled off again—or disappeared altogether.

"Where did you go?" Mrs. Villalobos said.

Luisa thought of the six shrouded corpses lying on a hill overlooking the village where they had lived, loved, and ultimately met their painful and untimely ends.

"I went to hell and back."

And she was about to make a return trip, this time by way of Santa Martha Jail.

"You look nice today. I like you better in regular clothes." Mrs. Villalobos ran a hand over the lapel of Luisa's blazer. "But why aren't you wearing your uniform?"

"I have an appointment this morning. I'll change before I head to the office."

Luisa had been wearing uniforms so long she felt more comfortable in them than she did "regular" clothes. She hadn't worn her police uniform to Agua Dulce because she hadn't wanted to put the villagers on the defensive any more than they already were. She hoped the tactic would have the same effect on Salvador Perez today. He had shut down the instant he had seen the Federal Police insignia on her uniform shirt. She hoped seeing her dressed like a yuppie instead of an authority figure would make him more willing to talk.

"What does your lady friend think about what you do for a living?" Mrs. Villalobos asked.

"Finn? We haven't talked about it much."

Luisa could tell Finn was anxious about the more dangerous aspects of her job. She wondered if her career could be a potential deal breaker if she and Finn could solve the logistics of living nearly two thousand miles and two time zones apart and try to form a relationship.

"Finn. That's an unusual name," Mrs. Villalobos said pensively. "What's her family name?"

"Chamberlain."

"Luisa Chamberlain doesn't have the same ring as Luisa Villalobos, but I suppose it will do in a pinch." Mrs. Villalobos flashed an impish grin. "You don't have to look so surprised. I've been around a while, but I'm hipper than I look."

To prove how hip she was, Mrs. Villalobos launched into a capable version of the Macarena, a dance that had reached its peak of popularity more than twenty years ago. Soon they were both out of breath, Mrs. Villalobos from dancing and Luisa from laughing at the impromptu performance.

"What was that for?" Mrs. Villalobos asked after Luisa kissed her on the cheek.

"I just wanted to thank you. After the day I had yesterday, I needed a good laugh to remind myself I still could."

"I'm glad I could help." Mrs. Villalobos cupped Luisa's cheek, then gave it a pat. "Tomorrow, I'll show you my version of *La Conquista*."

"Something to look forward to."

If Luisa remembered correctly, the folk dance Mrs. Villalobos had referred to was a retelling of Spanish soldiers' conquest of the Aztecs way back when. Dancers representing the soldiers usually wore modern clothes, but the ones representing the Aztecs wore feathers and dressed as eagle or jaguar warriors. All the dancers wore masks similar to the ones hanging in Mrs. Villalobos's apartment.

"Where are your people from, Mrs. Villalobos?"

The *Jarabe*, also known as the Mexican Hat Dance, was the national dance of Mexico, and was performed all over the country. *La Conquista* was more popular in the states of Jalisco and Michoacán.

"All over. My mother was from Guanajuato and my father was from Veracruz. My brother, my sisters, and I were born in Michoacán. I moved to Mexico City after I got married."

"Where does the rest of your family live?"

"My children and grandchildren are in Nayarit. Except for Javier. He decided to forge his own path," Mrs. Villalobos said proudly. "He moved east years ago. My brother and sisters lived in Michoacán all their lives. I've outlived them all. Javier says it's because I'm too tough to die. But enough of all this talk about me. If I tell you everything now, we won't have anything to talk about on Saturday." Mrs. Villalobos shooed her away. "Now go to work. You're already three hours late."

Luisa said her good-byes, then called Ruben when she reached the stairwell. She had turned the tire impressions over to him when they had returned to Mexico City in the wee hours of the morning. He had planned to head to the office early today so the guys in the forensics lab could give the molds the once-over and run them through their database.

"Do you have anything yet?" she asked.

"I just finished reading through the report. The tires came back as a match to a brand commonly found on 2012 Ford Suburbans."

Luisa knew the oversized SUV could seat up to nine. Perfect for ferrying a large family around—or a squad of hit men.

"Were any 2012 Suburbans spotted near Agua Dulce two days ago?"

"I called Miguel Serrano a few minutes ago," Ruben said. "He said no one has reported seeing one, but one was found abandoned and burned some forty miles away from his farm."

"So the hit men dumped the car on their way out of Agua

Dulce. Any prints, trace, or DNA we might have been able to obtain from it has gone up in smoke. Perfect. Was Miguel able to give you the VIN, at least?"

"Yeah. The vehicle identification number he provided ties the car to Idoia Ocampo."

Luisa used her shoulder to hold her phone against her ear while she grabbed a pen and recorded the name in her notebook.

"Do we have an address for her?"

"The P.O. box at a mailing center appears to be a legitimate address. The physical's a fake. I could tell you what it is, but I'm afraid it wouldn't do you much good."

"Tell me anyway."

When Ruben recited the address, Luisa recognized it right away. It belonged to one of the most famous tourist attractions in Mexico City—the Monument to the Revolution. The edifice was located near two of the major thoroughfares in the heart of the city and served as both a memorial commemorating the Mexican Revolution as well as a mausoleum for the remains of some of the heroes from the conflict. Luisa could see the century-old landmark from her apartment window. Was the leader of the Jaguars hiding right under her nose or was this part of the game of hide-and-seek he had been playing with authorities for years now?

"We're back at square one." Ruben blew out a sigh of frustration. "That family in Agua Dulce died for nothing because we're never going to catch this guy."

Luisa refused to accept the possibility that her search would prove as fruitless as Carlos Ramos's and all the others who had preceded him. Hundreds of innocent victims like Silvia Perez and her family deserved to be avenged, and she was determined to see them—and the leader of the Jaguars—receive the justice they were due.

"I won't stop looking until we find him, Ruben. Have someone watch the mail center to see if anyone picks up deliveries to the drop box, and talk to the manager to see if he or she can tell us anything about the box's owner. I'm headed to Santa Martha Jail to speak to Salvador Perez again. Call me if you hear anything."

"I will. Be careful."

"You, too."

Luisa ended the call and headed to the parking garage. She set her notebook on the trunk of her car and dropped to her hands and knees to check under the chassis. Thankfully, she didn't spot anything unusual. She turned when she heard footsteps behind her.

A professional-looking man wearing a suit that looked like it cost ten times as much as hers asked, "Is everything okay? Do you need some help?"

Luisa stood and dusted off her hands.

"No, I'm fine," she said with an embarrassed laugh. "I was just checking things out. Thanks, anyway."

Instead of walking away, the man took a step closer. His broad form filled the gap between her car and the one next to it, effectively penning her in.

"*El jefe* says hello."

In one smooth move, the man dropped his leather briefcase and flicked his wrist, revealing a knife with a retractable eight-inch blade. Then he lunged at her.

Luisa parried his thrust, using the heel of her hand to knock his arm away. She reached for her gun but couldn't clear it from its holster before he was on her again. She held up her left arm to ward him off and cried out when she felt the knife's sharp blade slice through her clothes and pierce her skin. Blood coursed from the wound, but she didn't have time to stop and inspect the damage.

She took a step back to give herself some distance. When the man advanced toward her, she turned sideways and drove his head into her windshield. As blood from his broken nose splattered on the glass, he dropped the knife and crumpled to the ground. Luisa kicked the knife away, cuffed the man to her front bumper, and called 066 for emergency police assistance. The connection was spotty because of all the concrete and reinforced steel surrounding her, but she was eventually able to relay her request for help.

"Haven't you heard?" she asked as her attacker began to stir. "You should never bring a knife to a gun fight."

He jerked at the handcuff on his wrist and let out an angry roar when he couldn't pull free. Luisa held her gun on him as she examined the ID in the wallet she had slipped from his pocket while he was unconscious. His driver's license said his name was Gilberto Ruiz and listed an address in Vicente Guerrero in the neighboring state of Tlaxcala.

"You came a long way to ruin my best suit, Gilberto Ruiz." Luisa pressed her palm against her left arm to staunch the bleeding. "Who sent you? Who's your boss?"

Gilberto pressed his lips together and shook his head like a toddler refusing to eat his vegetables.

"I don't talk to cops. Call my lawyer," he said as the approaching sirens of police cars and ambulances signaled the backup Luisa had called for was on the way. "I'm suing you for police brutality."

"Good luck finding anyone but a public defender to take your case once you're charged with the attempted murder of a Federal Police officer."

She held her gun and badge over her head to let the first responders streaming into the parking garage know she was on their side. She summarized the situation for them, then tossed a patrol officer the keys to her handcuffs. She needed to get going. She had to make her way to Santa Martha Jail to make sure Salvador Perez hadn't been targeted, too. Then she needed to sit down with Gilberto Ruiz and find out who had ordered him to kill her.

"Where do you think you're going?" The paramedic examining the cut on her arm clamped a latex glove-covered hand around her wrist. "You need stitches and a bandage. A tetanus shot wouldn't hurt, either."

"Do what you have to do," Luisa said impatiently. "Just make it fast. I've got somewhere I need to be."

The paramedic rolled his eyes. "Male or female, you cops are all alike."

She followed him to his rig and sat on a gurney while he tended to her wound.

"Moreno."

She looked up to find Gilberto Ruiz, his hands cuffed behind his back, glaring at her vindictively as he resisted the officers' attempts to put him in the back of their squad car. She tried not to tremble as she met his eye. His cold, unfeeling gaze had very nearly been the last thing she had seen. But his words struck even more fear into her heart than his dead-eyed stare.

"You're going to die today, bitch. You and everyone you love."

❖

After the tour bus pulled into the half-empty parking lot at the foot of the site containing the ruins of Chichén Itzá, Richard counted heads and handed out tiny red radios dangling from plastic lanyards.

"The radios should be tuned to channel twenty-three. If you place the earbuds in your ears, you will be able to hear me speak even if you decide to wander off on your own. The vendors you see here are only a few of the ones scattered around the site, which covers nearly two square miles. We will be here for two hours. You are free to spend your time as you wish—shopping or following me around the ruins. If you do go off on your own, please be sure to meet the rest of the group at the bus at noon. We will be heading back to the resort promptly at twelve fifteen. We should arrive around two thirty. Just in time for a late lunch. Any questions?"

Finn looked around, but no one raised her hand.

"Good. Let's go."

Finn and the rest of the group followed Richard through the gates. A short time later, they passed a restaurant and gift shop, modern additions that contrasted sharply with the ancient ruins they had come to see.

"An estimated one point two million tourists visit the ruins every year," Richard said. "We're here relatively early so the grounds shouldn't be too crowded. We'll probably have to share our stay with a few students on field trips, but we shouldn't have to deal with the masses of tourists that will be streaming in later in the day."

The temperature wasn't too bad yet, but Finn could feel it starting to rise. She took a sip of her bottled water so she could stay hydrated. Beside her, Ryan mirrored her action.

"The buildings of Chichén Itzá are grouped into a series of complexes," Richard said. "Today, we're going to focus on the best known. The Great North Platform includes the monuments of El Castillo, the Temple of Warriors, and the Great Ball Court. Directly ahead of you is El Castillo, also known as the Temple of Kukulkán."

He pointed to the pyramid that was the most recognizable of all the ruins in Chichén Itzá. The pre-Columbian structure stood ninety-eight feet tall and consisted of a series of nine square terraces. Each side of the pyramid featured a stairway that rose at a forty-five-degree angle. Finn was amazed by the ancient builders' ability to create such precise measurements using such primitive implements. Like the pyramids of Egypt, which she had also been privileged to see in person, the feat was an engineering marvel she couldn't wrap her head around even as she admired its beauty.

"I'll bet running those stairs would be a serious workout, especially in this heat," Ryan said.

"I doubt you'd get very far."

Finn indicated the ropes surrounding the base of the pyramid, barriers installed to prevent trespassers from inflicting damage to the centuries-old structure by enacting the exercise routine Ryan had just mentioned.

"Details."

"This pyramid was constructed in honor of the serpent god Kukulkán," Richard continued, speaking into the headset microphone transmitting his voice to the radios he had disseminated earlier. "Notice the snake heads at the base of the pyramid? During the spring and autumn equinoxes, the northwest corner of the pyramid casts shadows on the north balustrade that look like a serpent crawling down the stairs."

"Cool," Finn said as she snapped a few pictures.

"You really get into this stuff, don't you?" Ryan asked.

"Don't you?" Finn took another sip of water from her slowly dwindling supply. She reminded herself not to drink it too fast so she wouldn't run out before the end of the two-hour tour. "I mean, isn't that why you're here?"

Ryan looked sheepish.

"To be honest, I only signed up because Jill seemed so into it. We haven't spent much time together this week and I thought this outing would help us fix that. Then she changed her mind to watch wrestling, the only 'sport' I can't stand."

Finn smiled as she realized Jill's feelings for Ryan might not be quite so one-sided after all.

"I have a feeling she misses you, too."

"You think so?" Ryan asked hopefully.

"I know so."

Finn turned her attention back to Richard as he demonstrated El Castillo's peculiar acoustics. When he clapped his hands on one side of the pyramid, the echo sounded normal. On the other side, the reverberation sounded like the chirp of a native bird.

"Whose idea was it for you to try out for Friends and Lovers, Jill's or yours?" Finn asked.

Ryan screwed up her face as she slowly clapped her hands and tried to figure out the secret behind the odd echo.

"Mine," she said, abandoning her quest. "Our friends are always saying we're like an old married couple. Tonight gives us a chance to either prove or disprove the theory. Don't you have someone in your life like that? Someone who knows you better than you know yourself?"

Finn thought it over as they followed Richard and the rest of the group to the Great Ball Court, the largest and best preserved court of its kind. The playing area was more than five hundred fifty feet long, and the surrounding walls were twenty-six feet high. Rings carved with intertwined serpents were set high up in the center of each wall. At the base were sculpted stone panels inscribed with images of ball players. On one panel, one of the players had been decapitated, giving new meaning to the phrase "life-and-death-competition."

"I don't make friends easily," Finn said at length. "I've found that most situations tend to work out better for me if I don't let people get too close."

"You could have fooled me. You've been right in the middle of things all week, not on the outside looking in. Well, you started out that way, but you've been a social butterfly ever since."

Finn started to protest until she realized it was true. She had been forced to take some quiet time Monday morning, but she hadn't felt the need to repeat the ritual since. In fact, she had found herself looking forward to each day's long list of activities so she could see what she would do—and who she might meet—next. Would she still feel this way after she completed her story? When she got back to the "real world" in a few days, would she discover her newfound comfort was exclusive to this trip and the group of women sharing it with her, or would it follow her home?

"This week has been the exception rather than the rule."

She looked at the entrance to the Lower Temple of the Jaguar. The columns were covered in elaborate bas-relief carvings, and a worn Jaguar throne, also carved of stone, sat in the entrance.

"Why is that?" Ryan asked.

Finn felt a familiar sense of dread. How much should she reveal about herself? Should she tell Ryan everything or just enough to answer her question?

"I grew up in a small town in Montana," she said, reciting an oft-told tale. "Neighbors were few and far between. The few friends I had were people I'd known all my life. We attended the same one-room schoolhouse from the time we were eight years old until we graduated high school. I experienced serious shell shock when I got to college. I had never seen so many people gathered in one place at one time. I was used to having my neighbors live hundreds of acres away, not a few feet. Freshman year was rough. Every day felt like a test I hadn't adequately studied for. I survived, but I still prefer living in my own bubble in my own space."

"But you're in San Francisco now, right? There aren't many wide open spaces there."

"You'd be surprised. I work out of my apartment most of the time, so I don't have to deal with a commute. And even when I go out, there are plenty of places to choose from that aren't crawling with tourists. There's a pedestrian walkway on the Golden Gate Bridge that makes you feel like you're walking in the clouds, especially when the fog rolls in. There are also a ton of parks to choose from, and the Japanese Tea Garden is a great place to meditate. So, even in a city of millions, I can feel like I'm all alone."

"Don't you miss Montana?" Ryan asked as she slathered more sunscreen on her arms. "The pictures I've seen make it seem so beautiful there."

"It is. The views are some of the most amazing you can find in the whole country. But the nearest airport is a three-hour drive from my parents' house, which would make it extremely inconvenient for me to move back to my hometown and continue to travel as much as I do. Most of my family still lives in Montana. I go back to visit them a couple times a year. I enjoy the time I spend with them, but it doesn't feel like home anymore."

"I know how you feel. I love going home for the holidays each year, but I love returning to my own life even more. Since you seem to prefer your own company, I'm guessing a relationship is out of the question."

"Too many places to see. Too many things to do."

"You must save all the romance for your books because your life seems to have a distinct lack of it."

Finn started to protest but held her tongue because Ryan was right. She had sex—lots of it—but romance had always been a rarity in her life. Romance was more than a torrid affair or a brief hook-up. When was the last time she had bought a Valentine's Day card or received one in return? When was the last time she had viewed a relationship as something with the potential to be long lasting instead of temporary? Longer than she was willing to admit. But Luisa made her want to do all those things and more. Had her latest change of scenery caused her to have an unexpected change of heart?

She had felt a connection with Luisa from the moment they met. At the time, she'd thought the bond was only sexual. The time they'd spent exploring each other's bodies hadn't done much to disprove the theory. Over the past week, however, she had slowly discovered the connection she felt with Luisa was more than physical. It was emotional as well. And it seemed to be getting deeper every day. Now the accompanying feelings were too strong to ignore.

She and Luisa needed to talk. And not on the phone this time. They needed to talk face-to-face. And when they did, Finn needed to tell Luisa her whole story, not the airbrushed version she usually trotted out at parties. She needed to tell Luisa about her fear and uncertainty. All the things she usually tried to hide. Because in order to win Luisa's heart, she needed to show Luisa what was in hers.

Richard's voice drew Finn from her reverie.

"If you will follow me through the market, I'll take you to the Cenote Sagrado, the sinkhole that once provided water to the Mayans. It's a bit of a hike, but if you're up to the task, you'll be rewarded with shade at the end of the journey."

Finn and the rest of the tour group walked down a sloping dirt walkway. Vendors lined both sides. Their booths offered everything from T-shirts bearing screen-printed images of El Castillo to hand-knitted blankets depicting Mayan warriors in full battle dress to replica jerseys of the Mexican national soccer team's most popular players. Finn slowed in front of a booth laden with hand-carved treasures of all kinds: animal figurines, decorative masks, and tiny articulated skeletons in honor of the Day of the Dead.

The booth's owner, a slight young man in a Mickey Mouse T-shirt and designer knockoff skinny jeans, sat on an overturned five-gallon bucket. Finn stopped to watch him work. Wood shavings fell at his sneaker-clad feet as the rectangular block of wood in his hands slowly began to mimic the form of the crouching jaguar tattooed on his left forearm.

"Would you like to see my little shop?" he asked without looking up. "Everything one dollar. Practically free."

Finn didn't want to buy anything. She just wanted to watch him work. She raised her camera and took several pictures as the pile of wood shavings continued to grow. The vendor's hair fell into his eyes as he hunched over the carving, preventing Finn from getting any good shots of his face. She didn't mind, though, because his strong, skilled hands were his most memorable feature.

"Nice work," she said.

"Thank you, *señorita*."

"Are you coming, Finn?" Ryan asked.

"I'm right behind you."

Finn took one last photograph of the vendor before she left his booth to join Ryan standing near a pair of tourists haggling over the price of a ceramic replica of El Castillo. She and Ryan continued down the dirt path. A few minutes later, they joined the rest of their group in a wooded area overlooking a deep hole. Finn sighed at the drastic drop in temperature. She hoped Richard's upcoming lecture would be long-winded instead of brief. She wanted to enjoy the shade as long as she could before she resumed baking in the sun.

"The Sacred Cenote, *Cenote Sagrado* in Spanish, is also known as the Well of Sacrifice," Richard said. "The Mayans performed sacrifices, sometimes human, in honor of the rain god Chaac. When the cenote was dredged one hundred years ago, artifacts of jade, gold, pottery, and incense were discovered, along with human remains. As you can probably tell from what you've learned today, the average life span wasn't very long during the pre-Columbian period. In certain parts of the country, it still isn't. That's why I don't want my son to go into politics when he grows up. It's much too corrupt a profession. But that's just my opinion. You're free to disagree with me if you want."

"You've been right so far," one of the Barbies said. "Why stop now?"

"Madam, your check is in the mail." Richard bowed as deeply as a knight presenting himself to a monarch. "Now let's move on to El Caracol."

He led the group back through the cadre of vendors to a round building resting atop a square platform.

"If the building looks like an observatory," he said, "it should. Its windows and doors are aligned to track Venus's path as it crosses the sky."

"How could such a primitive society be so advanced?" Finn wondered aloud.

"Aliens," Ryan said. "They learned everything they knew from little green men from Mars. Men are from Mars and women are from Venus. Get it?"

Finn got the allusion but didn't find it quite as amusing as Ryan seemed to.

"Perhaps I should leave the jokes to the professionals."

"Perhaps."

They toured a few more ruins, then headed to the exit. The parking lot that had been practically deserted when they arrived was now filled with dozens of buses from various tour groups, resorts, and hotels. Finn looked for the bus labeled SOS Tours. Ryan spotted it first.

"There it is."

"I wonder what happened to our driver," Finn said after they boarded the bus and settled into their seats.

Leo, the man who had driven them from Cancún, was in his fifties. The man smoking in front of the bus was a good thirty years younger, though the black baseball cap pulled low over his forehead and the mirrored sunglasses covering his eyes made it difficult to guess his exact age.

"Too much sun, I imagine." Ryan adjusted the vent over her head so the chilled air could blow directly on her. "A few more minutes in that heat and I might have keeled over, too. Some fires I've fought haven't been as hot as it was today."

Richard counted heads to make sure each member of the group was present and accounted for. Some had veered off to go shopping instead of following the rest of the group around the grounds, but all had made it back to the bus on time.

"Show of hands." Richard raised his hand as if he was about to testify in court. "Who wants the air-conditioning lower, who wants it higher, and who thinks it's just fine as is?"

"Lower," everyone yelled.

"So much for a show of hands."

Richard picked up a large cardboard box and walked down the aisle carrying bags of potato chips. Finn opted for ruffled chips instead of plain. Ryan grabbed one of each.

"Where's Leo?" Finn asked as she opened her small bag of chips.

"He was called away on a family emergency. Our relief driver, Javier, will take us back to the resort. Let's go home, Javi."

Javier closed the bus's doors and slowly pulled out of

the crowded parking lot. Ryan's cell phone chimed as the bus picked up speed.

"It's probably Jill checking up on me to make sure I'll be getting back in plenty of time to do the show tonight."

Ryan wiped her hand on her shorts and dug her phone out of her pocket. The message she opened wasn't a text but a video. Jill's face filled the small screen.

"I wanted you to see what you're missing," Jill said. "Get a load of this."

On the screen, Jill's sunburned face was replaced by shots of two masked wrestlers beating the crap out of each other in an elevated ring set up where the craft table normally rested. Hundreds of cheering women were crowded around the ring. After a few minutes of high-flying action, the camera shifted to focus on two speedboats motoring into the lagoon. Instead of the shirtless resort workers Finn had seen piloting the boats all week, the vehicles were manned by ten men carrying assault rifles. Ten more armed men dressed in camouflage came running in from the beach.

"This is so cool," Jill said on the video. "These guys are really going all out. They've even got the *Federales* in on the act. Now don't you wish you had stayed?"

Something about the scene didn't feel right to Finn. The wrestlers were obviously pretending to fight, but the guys with the guns didn't seem like they were faking their aggression.

"I don't think this is part of the show, Ryan."

Ryan's face was pale beneath her tan.

"Neither do I."

They watched as a wrestler wearing a jaguar mask stood on the ring ropes and motioned for one of the newcomers to toss him a rifle. When he caught it and shot a volley of bullets into the air, the audience's cheers turned into screams. Some women rose from their seats and tried to run, but the men aimed their guns at them and ordered them to remain where they were.

The man in the jaguar mask peered at the panicked crowd as he slowly circled the square ring. "Which one of you is Finn Chamberlain?"

Ryan gasped when the screen went black.

"What was that about?" she asked, her face ashen. "Was it real? Why were those men looking for you?"

Finn's heart hammered in her chest. She didn't know who the men were. She didn't know why they were looking for her. And, most of all, she didn't know how they knew her name. She had always sought to fade into the background. Now she was being thrust in the spotlight. And she had no idea why.

"I'm—I'm nobody." She forced the words out as her mouth, throat, and tongue fought against her. "I'm just—I'm just a travel writer from San Francisco."

"Then what's all this about? How did those men know your name?"

"I—I—" Finn closed her eyes and ran through her rituals as she tried to control her stutter. She took several deep breaths and concentrated on slowing her speech. "I wish I knew," she finally managed to say. "Call Jill and see if she can tell us more. Before we go running off half-cocked, we need to know if what we saw was real."

"Good idea." Ryan hit speed dial. "If this is a prank, I'll kill her." She put the phone to her ear, then frowned and shook her head. "Straight to voice mail."

"Try again."

Ryan hit redial, then shook her head again. "Same thing. You don't think she's—"

"Don't go there," Finn said, even though she already had.

"What are we supposed to do?"

"I don't know. I'm just as lost as you are, if not more

so." She forced herself to think clearly, even though fear was clouding her thoughts. "Send me the video."

"What are you going to do, upload it to YouTube or something and hope it goes viral?"

"No, I'm going to forward it to someone who might be able to help us. Her name's Luisa Moreno. She's a Federal Police officer in Mexico City."

"How well do you know her?"

Finn had asked herself the same question a few days ago. Then, she had hoped the answer would ease her mind. Now it might save her life.

"Well enough."

"That was just a show, right?" Ryan's hands shook as she punched in Finn's cell number. "Just part of a show?"

"I hope so."

Finn desperately wanted to say yes, but she didn't dare. She kept her voice low and her face impassive to keep from alarming her fellow passengers—or Javier, who seemed to be using the rearview mirror to keep tabs on her instead of the trailing traffic. She surreptitiously eyed her phone as she waited for Ryan's text message to arrive.

"We're sitting right next to each other," she said, trying not to panic as the minutes crawled by and no notification for an incoming message appeared on her phone. "Why is it taking so long?"

"It's a pretty big file. Maybe it's taking a while to load. Give it a little while longer."

Finn loosed a sigh of relief when her phone finally chirped. She checked the message to make sure it was from Ryan instead of someone else, then pressed *Forward* and keyed in Luisa's cell phone number.

Four days ago, Luisa had told her there was nothing to worry about. She needed that same reassurance now.

"Come on, super cop," she said as she hit *Send*. "Tell me what I need to hear."

❖

No cell phones or outside weapons were allowed inside Santa Martha Jail, so Luisa stashed her cell phone and gun in the glove compartment of her car. She flinched after she slammed the compartment's door shut. Her left arm hurt from top to bottom. Her shoulder ached from the tetanus shot the EMT had given her, and her forearm throbbed where Gilberto Ruiz had slashed her.

You're going to die today, bitch, Ruiz had said before he was carted off to jail for processing. *You and everyone you love.*

She didn't know whether to take his threat seriously, but the risk of ignoring it was one she wasn't willing to take. On her way to Santa Martha Jail, she had called her family in Dallas to make sure they were safe. She hadn't told them what was going on because she didn't want them to worry if there was no reason to. Ruiz was apparently acting under orders, but whose? She couldn't tell her family they could be at risk until she knew where the danger was coming from.

Her mother had said she felt better just hearing Luisa's voice. Luisa felt better knowing her family was out of the narcos' reach. Allegedly. Drugs crossed the border every day and managed to go undetected. A hit man could easily follow the same route if his boss's pockets—and thirst for revenge—were deep enough to fund the effort.

The Federal Police didn't have jurisdiction north of the border, but Luisa had a few friends on the Dallas police force who said they would keep their eyes peeled for any signs of danger.

But who would protect her? She was out here on her own with no one to watch her back. No matter. She had a job to do.

She scanned the visitors' parking lot. Seeing no one who seemed to be lying in wait for her, she got out of her car and headed inside the jail, where she signed the visitors' log and showed her badge to the officer behind the desk.

"Luisa Moreno from the Federal Police. I'm here to meet with Salvador Perez."

The log was divided into three columns: Date, Visitor's Name, and Prisoner's Name. She scanned the list of names to see if Salvador Perez's name was listed and who might have come to see him. Fortunately or unfortunately—she couldn't decide which—her search came up empty.

The officer came around the desk and patted her down, then waved her on.

"We've set you up in interview room number three," he said. "It's the second door on your right. Go in and have a seat. The guards will bring the prisoner in shortly."

On her previous visit to the jail, Luisa had attempted to speak with Salvador Perez over the phone through a thick pane of glass. Surrounded by nearly a dozen other prisoners having conversations with their lawyers and loved ones, Perez hadn't had much to offer other than advice on the myriad ways she could go fuck herself.

The surroundings for their second meeting had changed. The circumstances had as well. Would Perez continue to keep the secrets of an organization that wanted them both dead, or had the brutal murders of his family managed to convince him to share what he knew?

She placed her notebook and a small tape recorder on the table and waited for Perez to arrive. She pressed *record* when the door opened. Perez came into the room with a guard holding on to each arm. Shackles around his ankles forced him to shuffle rather than walk. The handcuffs around his wrists were secured to a thick chain wrapped around his waist, preventing him from raising his arms more than a few inches. The guards forced him into a metal chair and secured him in place by cuffing his hands to a metal bar bolted to the table and his feet to a thick ring secured to the floor.

"You're crazy if you think I'm going to talk to you," Perez said. "Talking to you is what got my whole family killed."

"I didn't get a chance to speak with the members of your family, Salvador. They were dead before I made it to Agua Dulce. Are you going to tell me who killed them, or should I wait for Gilberto Ruiz to take you out, too?"

Perez's left eye twitched. Luisa had expected the mention of Ruiz's name to elicit a reaction, though she hadn't expected one quite so visceral.

"We arrested him this morning after he gave me this." Luisa indicated the bandage around her arm. "If you ask the guards nicely, maybe the two of you can be cell mates after he's processed."

"You can't do that. Ruiz is a stone cold killer. I'm just a…"

Perez's voice trailed off. The guilty expression on his face was almost comical. If Luisa had caught him doing something other than indirectly admitting to having ties to the Jaguars' organization, she might have laughed.

"You're just a what? A wannabe? A little boy pretending to be a big man? After you spend a few hours with Gilberto Ruiz, we'll see if you're ready for the big time."

Luisa slammed her notebook shut and rose from the table. Perez lunged toward her but, thanks to being cuffed in place, he didn't get far.

"Wait."

He stretched his hands as far as he could, pleading for her not to go.

Luisa resumed her seat.

"Do you have something you want to say to me?"

"I'm dead if I help you, and I'm dead if I stay in here."

Perez balled his hands into fists. He looked like an animal caught in a trap. So desperate to escape he would gnaw off his own extremities if it meant he could find freedom.

"Then tell me who I'm looking for. Who's the leader of the Jaguars? What does he look like? Where does he live?"

"I only know what I need to know. I take orders from a guy who takes them from someone else. Even the guy they fear the most isn't the one in charge. He's just taking orders like everybody else."

"Names, Salvador. Give me names." Luisa spread the photos of the four unidentified men on the table. "Who are they?" She tapped one of the photos with her finger. "This one has the same ink across his stomach that you do. Did you know him, or do you simply want to be him when you grow up? A nameless corpse with no one left to mourn him."

He laughed bitterly. "Thanks to you, I already am."

Luisa fought down a wave of guilt.

"Your family's deaths are on your head, not mine, Salvador. They died because someone wanted to intimidate you into keeping his identity safe. What are you hoping to receive in return, a hefty payment for your loyalty? You're more likely to get shanked in the shower or, if you're lucky enough to make it out of here, shot execution-style in a back alley the second you hit the street."

Perez stared at her wordlessly. He put up a good front, but she could see his façade starting to crumble.

"Like you said, you're dead if you stay and you're dead

if you go. If you keep following the path you're on, your life won't be worth anything. But if you help me, you'll have meaning. Help me, Salvador."

"You're making me out to be some kind of hero. Where I come from, snitches ain't heroes. Even if I did help you find who you're looking for, how are you going to protect me? You can't even protect yourself."

He let his eyes drift to the bandage on her arm, but Luisa didn't take hers off his face.

"Why did you ask me to stay if all you plan to do is sit here and waste my time? Perhaps I should be talking to Gilberto Ruiz instead. Maybe he'll be more willing to make a deal than you are."

Director Chavez himself was on his way to interview Ruiz. Ruiz had been through this song and dance so many times Luisa suspected he was too tough to break. She hoped Perez wouldn't see through her bluff.

Tears welled in Perez's eyes and slowly rolled down his cheeks. He tried to knuckle them away, but his hands couldn't reach that far.

"If I knew something, don't you think I'd tell you?" He turned his face toward the wall, too embarrassed to show he wasn't as heartless as he pretended to be. "My little sister was only four years old. When I think about what they did to her and the rest of my family…" His chains rattled against the table as his body shook with sobs. "I don't know who the fucking leader of the Jaguars is. I can't help you, Officer. I wish I could."

Luisa waited for him to regain his composure before she tried again.

"Do you know who any of these men are?" she asked, indicating the photographs laid out before him.

Perez wiped his runny nose on his shoulder.

"The one with the tat? He's my uncle, Marcos. When I was a kid, I wanted to be just like him one day. He had it all. Money, cars, plenty of bitches—I mean women. When I turned sixteen, he introduced me to a guy he said could get me paid. I started doing some work for him."

"What was the man's name?"

"Hernan Cisneros," he said, naming the low-level dealer who had been arrested sitting on a five-million-dollar stash. "Hernan said if I worked hard, I could move up. He said he thought I could be a hitter like my uncle."

"By hitter, you mean hit man?"

Perez nodded.

"Hitters have jaguar tattoos on their left forearm. They get one after they make their first kill. When I saw that bandage on your arm, I thought you might be one of us. But you can't be because you're still alive. When a hitter betrays the Jaguars, they kill him and cut off his tattoo. Except the tattoo comes off before he dies, not after, so he can feel the pain."

"Is that what happened to your uncle and the rest of these men?"

Perez nodded again.

"Hernan killed my uncle and the other guys in those pictures because word came down from on high that they couldn't be trusted to keep their mouths shut about who they worked for. My uncle liked to party. When he got too much mescal in his system, he liked to talk. A lot. Those other guys were the same way."

"Did Hernan remove their tattoos?"

"He said the boss told him they didn't deserve to wear them anymore. He tied each of them to a chair, peeled off their tats, and shot them in the head. When he was done, he was supposed to toss their bodies in a fifty-gallon drum, douse them with gas, and burn them, but I guess he either got lazy or ran out of time."

Luisa scribbled furiously in her notebook. Even though the conversation was being recorded, she preferred to track it the old-fashioned way.

"What else did Hernan say?"

"That the boss knows all and sees all and we shouldn't expect to get away with anything or the Carver would make us pay."

"The Carver?" That was a new name. She hadn't seen it mentioned in any of Carlos Ramos's case files. She wrote it down and underlined it for emphasis. "Who's the Carver?"

Perez shrugged. "Someone I never hope to meet."

Luisa grilled him for another thirty minutes, but he didn't reveal anything else of note. Instead of heading directly to the office, she stuck around the parking lot hoping to touch base with Director Chavez first. She wanted to know what, if anything, he was able to glean from his interrogation of Gilberto Ruiz.

While she waited, she sat in her car and tried to wrap her head around everything Perez had told her. She felt like she was trying to put a jigsaw puzzle together. She had assembled the pieces that formed the frame, but she couldn't get the ones in the middle to fit.

She checked her watch. Twelve thirty. Finn should be on her way back from Chichén Itzá. She decided to call her now instead of waiting until tonight.

"Hopefully, her day was better than mine."

When she powered up her phone and saw the video Finn had sent her, she realized her day was about to get much worse.

❖

Finn had set the ringer on her phone to vibrate so she wouldn't draw any more attention from the relief bus driver than she was already receiving. She brought her cell to her ear when it buzzed in her hand.

"Luisa? Thank God."

"Finn, what's going on?" Luisa's voice sounded concerned but calm. Free of the growing panic that was gripping Finn by the throat. "Are you all right?"

"I'm alive. That's all I can say for now. Did you get the video I sent you?"

"That's why I'm calling."

"Is it real?" Finn asked. Her heart rate kicked up a few more notches as she waited for the answer.

"I don't know yet. Several guests and employees from some of the neighboring properties reported hearing gunshots coming from the Mariposa. The resort's head of security called the local police station to say everything was fine and the gunshots were part of some kind of exhibition being put on for the guests. As a precaution, local police were dispatched to check things out for themselves."

"What did they find?" Finn gripped Ryan's hand as they tried to offer each other support.

"They haven't reported back yet."

Ryan squeezed Finn's hand to get her attention, then arched her eyebrows inquisitively. Her shoulders drooped in defeat when Finn shook her head to indicate Luisa didn't have any more information about what was going on at the Mariposa than they did.

"I'm scared, Luisa. How did those people know my name? What could they possibly want from me?"

"If I'm right, they're using you to get to me. Remember the Jaguars, the drug cartel you asked me about earlier in the week? I'm getting close to finding out who their leader is, but someone doesn't want me to get any closer. They're going after me and everyone I care about."

"Some drug dealer wants to k-k-kill me to send you a m-m-message?" Finn pinched the bridge of her nose as she tried to remain focused. "How does he know you and I knew each other?"

"I don't know. I haven't mentioned you to anyone. No one except the woman who lives across the hall from me, but I can't see her being involved in this in any way. These guys are good. Someone must have seen us in Dallas and put two and two together. Where are you now?"

"On the bus. I know what road we're on, but I can't see a mile marker."

"That's okay. If I have to, I can use the cell towers to track your phone. Keep it powered on just in case. Are you headed back to the resort?"

"Yes. We left Chichén Itzá a little while ago, and we're supposed to arrive at the Mariposa by two thirty. I have to admit I'm afraid to see what we might find when we get there."

She couldn't stop imagining what might have happened at the resort after Jill's video went black. She hated to consider the awful possibility that the terrible images in her head might have actually come to pass.

"Everything's going to be fine, Finn, but let's focus on one thing at a time, okay? Did anything unusual happen during your trip?"

"Aside from receiving a video showing a group of armed m-m-men taking over my hotel and holding everyone inside h-h-hostage?"

"Focus, Finn," Luisa said, gently but forcefully bringing her back to the subject at hand. "Focus and breathe."

Finn felt her nerves begin to settle. How did Luisa know exactly what to say to help her control her stutter? Another question to ask her when this nightmare was over.

"Did anything happen in Chichén Itzá?" Luisa asked. "Did you see anyone or anything out of the ordinary? Anyone who might be following you?"

Finn glanced at Javier, who again seemed to be staring at her.

"Everything was fine on the first half of the trip, but we changed drivers for the return trip and the new one gives me the creeps. He keeps looking at me and I don't know why."

"What does he look like?"

"He's Mexican. Short. Skinny. Dark hair. He kind of looks like one of the vendors I saw selling figurines in the market at the site, but I can't say for sure. I wish I had paid more attention to his face than his hands."

"Don't beat yourself up. Take a look at him now and let me know if you think he's the same man you saw earlier."

Finn took a harder look at Javier. If she took away the baseball cap and sunglasses, he was a dead ringer for the man she had seen carving a jaguar from a block of wood.

"He's wearing long sleeves now, so I can't tell if he has a tattoo on his arm, but I think it's the same guy."

"Was the tattoo of a jaguar?"

"Yes. How did you know?"

"Lucky guess." Luisa had gasped when Finn confirmed what type of tattoo the man had. She sounded really excited now. "Do you know his name?"

"Our guide said his name was Javier."

"Javier what?"

"Richard didn't say."

"Can you take a picture of Javier without him seeing you do it?"

"I already did. I took several back at Chichén Itzá when I was watching him work. I planned to use them for my story. Wait. Those pictures are on my camera, not my phone. I can't access them without a computer."

She looked around the bus, but no one seemed to be pecking away on a laptop. Why would they? They were supposed to be on vacation, after all. A nice, relaxing escape from the troubles and pressures of the real world. So much for that.

"Hold on. Let me see if I can get another photo."

She leaned into the aisle. Javier seemed to be looking at the road instead of her for a change. She quickly snapped a shot of his face in the bus's oversized rearview mirror and ducked back into her seat.

"Did you get it?" she asked after she forwarded the photo to Luisa.

"Yes. It's uploading now." Luisa paused, then inhaled sharply. "Shit."

"What's wrong?"

"I think I just solved a mystery. I need to talk to my boss ASAP. Hold tight and let me know if anything changes. I'll call you back as soon as I can, okay?"

Finn could practically hear the adrenaline coursing through Luisa's veins. It sounded as loud as waves crashing in the ocean. "Luisa?"

"Yes?"

"Should I be worried?"

The length of time Luisa took to answer her question told Finn everything she needed to know.

"I'm going to get you out of this, *mariposa*. I promise."

Finn bit her lip to keep from crying. She had been in dangerous situations many times before on her trips, but she had never felt as close to death as she did now.

"*Ya'aburnee*. Do you remember what that means?"

"I remember," Luisa said softly. "It means 'you bury me.' But that's not going to happen. No one I love is going to die today. That includes you, Finn. I have to go, but I will call you back, okay?"

"Okay." Finn knew she couldn't stay on the phone much longer without raising Javier's suspicion, but she was reluctant to let go of her only lifeline. "Luisa?"

"Yes?"

"I love you, too."

And when this ordeal was over, she hoped to be able to say it to her face.

❖

One of Luisa's favorite guilty pleasures was action movies. The mindless car chases, countless gun battles, and laughter-inducing dialogue were as filled with empty calories as the popcorn she devoured while she watched them. Her favorite male action star was Jason Statham. In one of his early movies, he played a hit man who had to keep his adrenaline flowing or he would die. She needed hers to stop if she wanted Finn, everyone on the bus, and the women trapped inside the Mariposa Resort to live.

She took several deep breaths to try to get her nerves under control, but her nerves started jangling again as soon as she tried to figure out how she was supposed to be in three places at once. She needed to question Mrs. Villalobos to see if her suspicions about her were correct, she needed to be in Tinúm to intercept the bus Finn was riding in, and she needed to be in Cancún so she could help rescue the women who were being held hostage.

But where was she supposed to start? If she didn't get to

her apartment building in time, Mrs. Villalobos might escape and establish a false identity somewhere else. If she didn't send someone to stop the bus, Javier could pull over and slaughter everyone on it. And if local law enforcement wasn't able to penetrate the Jaguars' defenses at the Mariposa, they could have a bloodbath on their hands.

She radioed Director Chavez, told him her interview with Salvador Perez had been unsuccessful, and asked him to meet her at a coffee shop not too far from her apartment.

"What's going on, Moreno?" he asked after he arrived.

"I didn't mean to be deceptive, sir, but I didn't want to say too much over the air in case our transmissions are being monitored. Have you seen this?"

She thrust her phone into his hands and showed him the video of the attack on the Mariposa.

"Some of these look like our guys," he said, disappointment etched on his face. "Has this been confirmed?"

"Not yet. We're still waiting for local law enforcement to respond."

"If you haven't heard from them by now, chances are you aren't going to. They've most likely been killed or paid off by now. We need to get our troops in the air and on the ground as soon as possible."

She grabbed his beefy arm before he could rise from his seat.

"Wait. There's more. Finn Chamberlain, the woman who sent me the video, is on a bus traveling from Chichén Itzá. The driver is this man." She showed him the picture Finn had sent her. "His name is Javier Villalobos. I think he's the top enforcer for the Jaguars and he's been ordered to kill Finn to coerce me into ending my investigation."

"How many people are on the bus?"

"Thirty-nine passengers, a guide, and the driver."

"Forty potential witnesses." Director Chavez grimaced. "I doubt he plans to leave any of them behind. What are you suggesting we do? Try to save forty people and leave the countless others at the resort to die?"

"No, of course not. If we cut off the head of the snake, the body will die. I know who the leader of the Jaguars is. Before we take her in, maybe we can convince her to call the whole thing off."

"Are you saying the man we've been looking for all this time is a woman? Who?"

"Her name is Ines Villalobos. She's been right under our noses this entire time."

"How do you know it's her?"

"Javier Villalobos is her grandson. I saw his picture in her apartment and can say without a doubt he is the man driving Finn's bus. Based on what Salvador Perez told me, I have reason to believe Javier is the Carver, Ines's second-in-command. The owner of the car tied to the hit men who killed Perez's family is Idoia Ocampo. Ruben Huerta texted me a few minutes ago. He was able to identify Idoia Ocampo as Ines Villalobos's sister. Mrs. Ocampo died five years ago, three years before the vehicle she allegedly owns was purchased and four years before the local post office box attributed to her was opened. There have been several other big-ticket items purchased in her name after her death as well. Ines Villalobos has apparently been using her deceased sister's identity to launder money and run her operations."

"Ruben uncovered all that?" Director Chavez asked. "His skills are being wasted in Records. I need to move him up to our floor and pair him with you full-time. The two of you make a good team." He leaned forward, obviously intrigued by her recitation of facts. "What else do you have?"

Luisa didn't look down at her notes because she didn't need to refer to them in order to conclude her tale.

"Ines Villalobos's apartment is filled with jaguar-related memorabilia, which I initially thought were a nod to her Mayan heritage but are actually clues to her secret identity. Most of the evidence I've found to tie her to the case is circumstantial, I know, but there is one last thing. When Gilberto Ruiz tried to kill me this morning, he said everyone I loved was going to die today. The only person who knows I'm involved with Finn Chamberlain is Ines Villalobos."

Luisa normally tried to be circumspect about her personal life, but she hadn't thought twice when Mrs. Villalobos had pressed her for details about her fledgling relationship with Finn. Could one slip of the tongue cost her everything?

"It can't hurt to talk to the Villalobos woman and see what she says," Director Chavez said. "If you're right, you'll look like a genius. If you're wrong…"

"It could cost me my career. As long as it saves lives, it's a price I'm willing to pay."

"This is your op, Moreno. Tell me how you want to run it."

"Let's take your car. Mrs. Villalobos watches the street constantly and would have no problems recognizing my vehicle. I don't have any reason to come home this early in the day, so spotting me entering the building would raise her suspicions. I don't want her to know we're coming. Your windows are tinted dark enough that she won't be able to see inside even if she spots your car. Once we get inside, I'll run point and you can back me up. How long has it been since you've climbed three flights of stairs?"

He patted his round belly. "About twenty pounds ago, but don't worry about me, Moreno. I've got your back."

❖

Finn's anxiety continued to grow the longer she went without word from Luisa.

"When did she say she'd call you back?" Ryan asked.

"As soon as she could. It hasn't been that long."

"It's been half an hour. We'll be back at the hotel in ninety minutes. Then what? They gun us all down at the same time? We've got to do something. If this guy is as dangerous as your friend says he is, there's no way he's letting any of us make it off this bus alive."

Finn didn't want to admit Ryan might be right.

"Maybe we should get Richard involved and ask him to help us."

"But what if he's in on it, too? He knows this guy by name and must have worked with him before if he was willing to let him take over after Leo split. Until we know which side everybody's on, we can't trust anyone. I tell you one thing, though. If today's my day to die, I'm not going down without a fight."

"What do you have in mind?"

"We could rush him," Ryan said. "He can't take us all on at once. Wesley and LeeAnne are school bus drivers. One of them could take the wheel after we take Javier out."

Finn thought it over. The plan was risky, but if they got enough women to buy into it, it might work. As long as they weren't afraid of getting hurt. Perhaps even killed. The bus's aisles were so narrow two people couldn't stand side by side. They would have to make their run single file, which meant the women who volunteered to be at the front of the line would be in the most danger.

"Are you in?" Ryan asked.

"Yeah, I'm in."

Instead of waiting for Luisa to save her, perhaps it was time for her to save herself.

❖

Luisa knocked on Mrs. Villalobos's apartment door and moved out of the potential line of fire.

"Mrs. Villalobos, it's Luisa. May I come in?" She waited for a response. Hearing none, she knocked again. "Mrs. Villalobos?"

Director Chavez drew his gun.

"One more," he whispered. "Then I knock the door down."

He had obviously been watching the same movies she had. They could have asked the building manager to unlock the door for them, but she hadn't wanted to bring him into the situation in case he was on the Jaguars' payroll. She hadn't seen him when she entered the building, but had he seen her and Director Chavez and alerted Mrs. Villalobos that they were coming?

After she knocked on the door a third time, Director Chavez waved her out of the way so he could hurl himself against it.

"Ines Villalobos, this is Director Arturo Chavez with the Federal Police. Officer Moreno and I are coming in."

He aimed his attack at the door's hinges, which easily tore loose from the frame. The door canted to one side, then fell in with a crash.

Luisa scanned the room. On the TV, images from security cameras aimed at the interior and exterior of the building—and, she realized with a start, inside her own apartment—flickered across the screen.

She felt sick. She had moved into the building less than a

week ago and she already needed to move out. She had treated her apartment like a sanctuary. Her refuge from the dangers that awaited her outside its walls. How ironic was it that the one place she had felt safe had actually been where she had been most vulnerable?

She moved further into the room. The chair in front of the TV and the one in front of the window were empty because Mrs. Villalobos was sitting on the windowsill. Her feet and legs were inside the apartment, but her upper body was angled toward the ground thirty feet below. She gripped the sides of the window with both hands, ready to pull herself inside or push herself out into space.

Luisa holstered her gun and raised her hands.

"Come back inside, Mrs. Villalobos," she said as Director Chavez radioed for additional units. "We just want to talk to you."

Mrs. Villalobos smiled. "You're a clever girl, Luisa. From the minute I laid eyes on you, I knew you would be the one. Carlos Ramos came close to figuring everything out, but not as close as you."

"What happened to him?" Luisa asked as she slowly moved forward. "Did you have him killed?"

Mrs. Villalobos looked insulted.

"*Have* him killed? Silly girl, I took care of him myself."

"How?" Luisa tried to keep her talking. The longer she could keep the conversation going, the lower the likelihood the situation might end badly.

"I invited him over for dinner. Unfortunately, something in my *chilaquiles* didn't agree with him."

Luisa swallowed hard, wondering if she would have found Mrs. Villalobos's *tamales* just as disagreeable in two days' time.

"What did you do with Ramos's body?" she asked.

"I wrapped him in a rug and had two of my men throw him out like trash," Mrs. Villalobos said matter-of-factly.

Luisa looked at the area rug in the living room. She had been drawn to the bright colors the first time she visited Mrs. Villalobos's apartment. Now she knew why the rug had caught her eye. It wasn't as worn as the rest of the furniture and accessories in the apartment because Mrs. Villalobos had been forced to replace it after she used it to cover up the murder of Carlos Ramos.

"He's probably buried under tons of garbage in a landfill somewhere," Mrs. Villalobos said with a cruel smile. "Unless, of course, he was dumped in a fifty-gallon drum filled with gas and set on fire. It's hard to say. As you're well aware, my men can be rather creative sometimes."

Out of the corner of her eye, Luisa saw Director Chavez slowly circling around the left side of the room. She moved right, hoping she could distract Mrs. Villalobos long enough for Director Chavez to move close enough to grab her and pull her back inside.

"It's all over, Mrs. Villalobos. We have two of your men in custody and one is already talking. We know about Javier. We know about the attack on the Mariposa. And we know about you. We know everything. So please come quietly and—"

"Do what? Spend what's left of my life in prison? No."

Mrs. Villalobos shook her head so hard she nearly lost her grip. Luisa held her breath and Director Chavez stopped in his tracks, both waiting to see if Mrs. Villalobos would regain her balance or continue to lose it.

"You can make a deal," Luisa said after Mrs. Villalobos settled back into place. "You can make things easier on yourself."

"How?"

The look of curiosity on Mrs. Villalobos's creased face gave Luisa hope she might be getting through to her.

"Call Javier and your men at the Mariposa and tell them to stand down. Whatever you have planned for today, call it off."

"And you'll cut me a deal?"

Luisa wasn't authorized to make any offers. She turned to Director Chavez, hoping he would take the lead.

"Yes, I'll cut you a deal," Director Chavez said. "I will be happy to work with you as long as you work with us."

Mrs. Villalobos slowly reached into the pocket of her housedress. Luisa and Director Chavez trained their guns on her in case she drew a weapon of her own. Mrs. Villalobos pulled out a cell phone and punched in a number.

"Javier, it's me." Mrs. Villalobos looked up and met Luisa's eye. "Kill them all."

She let the phone drop and released her grip on the window. Her feet flew into the air as gravity tugged her toward the ground.

"No," Luisa cried.

Director Chavez made a desperate lunge but managed to grab only air.

Luisa heard screams and honking horns from passersby as Mrs. Villalobos's body hurtled toward the street.

"You were right." Director Chavez sounded as stunned as she felt.

"Yes, but what do we do now? Our best chance to end this mess just threw herself out that window."

Director Chavez pushed himself to his feet.

"Call Forensics. I want a team to go over every inch of this place to see if even a shred of Carlos Ramos's DNA is in here. Tell them to bring an electronics expert, too, so we can search her phone, security system, and anything else she might have around here. We need to identify who the other members of her organization are and where the money is. Ruiz may be able to help with that. He'll probably start singing like a bird as soon as he finds out his boss is dead. While you're doing that, I'll call the captains of the Yucatán and Quintana Roo state police forces and get them to send some troopers after the tour bus. They should be able to pen Villalobos in and take him down before he hurts anyone."

"And then?"

He placed a heavy hand on her shoulder.

"Pack your riot gear. You and I are going to Cancún."

The Federal Police had seventeen thousand patrol cars and dozens of planes and helicopters at its disposal. Troops could be in Cancún in a matter of hours. But when they arrived, Luisa feared, it might already be too late.

❖

The women sitting near Finn and Ryan had overheard most of their conversation. It didn't take long to bring the others up to speed, one whispered conversation at a time. Some were alarmed, naturally, but most managed to keep their cool.

Finn felt a buzz in the air. Tension. Excitement. Camaraderie.

She checked her watch. One thirty. Only an hour away from the resort. They had sixty minutes to put their plan into action. If Javier had an automatic weapon, he could mow them all down when they tried to rush him. But if they somehow managed to take him by surprise, they would be home free—as long as they didn't end up sending the bus careening off the road or into oncoming traffic.

"Are you ready?" Ryan asked.

"Give me a minute." Finn's phone vibrated while she was

trying to build up her courage for what needed to be done. She checked the display. "It's my editor," she said for Ryan's benefit. She pressed *Accept* and brought the phone to her ear. "Brett? What's going on?"

"I should ask you the same thing. I sent you to Cancún to cover a story. I didn't send you to *become* the story."

"You know what's going on?"

"A bunch of female tourists held captive by one of the most notorious drug cartels in Mexico? It's breaking news on all the major networks. I thought it was a hoax or, at worst, the opening line of a very bad joke. Now I know it's true. Are you all right?"

"For now."

Finn knew she shouldn't have been so surprised to hear that word had already trickled back to the States about her plight. Jill wasn't the only person at the resort with a cell phone. She—or someone else—must have reached out to the media to let them know what was happening. Was that what Javier and the rest of his cohorts wanted? To have the eyes of the world upon them? The real question was now that they had everyone's attention, how did they plan to exploit it?

"What do you need me to do?" Brett asked.

Finn almost laughed at the absurdity of the question. "This situation is a lot different than trying to put the next issue of the magazine to bed. I know you're used to being in charge instead of leaving the decisions to someone else, Brett, but I'm afraid there's nothing you can do."

"You know me. I can't sit around with my thumb up my ass. That would be a fate worse than—" Brett caught herself before she said the word Finn didn't want to hear. Especially now. "Stay safe."

"I'll do my best, but I'm afraid that's out of my hands."

Tears stung Finn's eyes as she considered everything she might be about to lose. Including her life. "Thanks for everything."

"Don't say that. It sounds too much like good-bye."

That's because it is.

"I've got to go," Finn said. "I'm expecting another call."

"Finn, don't hang—"

Finn ended the call before the emotion she heard in Brett's voice made her break down completely. She was barely holding on as it was. Her tenuous grip on reality was slipping by the second. It wouldn't take much to push her over the edge. When her phone rang again, she thought it might be Brett calling back to get in the last word. The perks of being the boss. When she looked down, however, she didn't see Brett's name or number on the screen. "It's Luisa."

Ryan turned toward her and leaned forward, her body language tense and her face fraught with anxiety. "Well, answer it."

Finn hoped Luisa had the answers she, Ryan, and the rest of the group so desperately needed to hear.

"Luisa? What did you find out?"

"Hold tight, *mariposa*. Help is on the way. State troopers are coming to intercept the bus. They should be there any minute now."

As soon as Luisa said the words, Finn heard sirens. Far off at first, but growing steadily closer. Ryan and the rest of the women cheered when the police cars pulled even with the bus and flanked it on all sides.

"Take that, fuckhead," Ryan said as she flipped Javier the bird.

"The police are here," Finn said.

"Talk me through it," Luisa said. "Tell me what's happening."

"The car in front is pumping his brakes to try to get Javier to slow down."

A clash of bumpers made Finn pitch forward. Her shoulder slammed into the back of the seat in front of her. She managed to turn her head in time to avoid a broken nose, but not a nasty case of whiplash.

"What happened, Finn?" Luisa asked. "Are you still there? Tell me what's going on?"

"Javier rammed the police car in front of the bus and ran it off the road."

Finn craned her sore neck to look behind her. The car had come to a stop in the median, parts of its rear end strewn along the road. The troopers inside looked pissed but unhurt.

"That was close," she said. Then her relief gave way to confusion. "Wait. Where are they going? Three of the cars flanking us just peeled off and roared ahead."

"If the traffic in front of you has been cleared, they're probably setting up for a roadblock."

"That's not going to stop him. If he's crazy enough to ram a police car, he's crazy enough to plow through a roadblock."

Richard, who had seemed paralyzed by fear after the police cars showed up, finally found his voice.

"Javi, stop. This is suicide."

"Yes, yours."

When Richard took a step toward him, Javier opened the bus's door, grabbed Richard by his collar, and shoved him outside. Finn watched as Richard tumbled across the pavement like a discarded rag doll. The remaining police cars on the right side of the bus swerved to miss him, then the drivers turned back to offer aid.

"Javier just threw our guide off the bus. We're going sixty miles an hour and he just—he just—"

Finn was too shaken by what she had just seen to finish her sentence.

Javier closed the bus's doors and turned to glare at his passengers.

"If anyone else has any bright ideas, they get to go for a ride next," he said in heavily accented English. "Do I have any takers?"

Finn heard whimpering as some of the women started to cry. Javier stepped on the gas as the bus neared the three police cars parked across the road.

"He's going to ram the roadblock."

Finn braced herself for impact. Seconds before there would have been a collision, the police car in the middle cleared out and allowed the bus to pass through the barricade unscathed. On the other side was nothing but open road. Javier headed straight for it. And no one was on his tail.

"Why aren't they coming for us, Luisa?" Finn asked. "Are they just going to let him go?"

"The troopers have decided it's too dangerous to attempt an interception. They don't want to risk anyone else getting hurt. They're going to follow you from a safe distance until your bus arrives at the hotel."

Luisa sounded frustrated as well as disappointed. Finn felt the same way. She also felt confused. And very, very afraid.

"Then what?" she asked. "They just w-w-wash their hands of us?"

"No. Calm down, Finn, and try to breathe. Is that better?" Luisa asked after Finn did as instructed.

"Yes."

"Okay. Now listen carefully. The state guys from Quintana Roo have the resort surrounded, and Director Chavez and I are heading to the airport now to bring reinforcements. We should land in about three hours. Stay strong, *mariposa*. I'm coming for you."

Finn hoped Luisa would arrive in time, but she didn't see how she could. Unless the Federal Police had a plane that could break the speed of sound, Luisa and her fellow officers would land in Cancún a good two hours after the bus returned to the resort. Then they would have to secure ground transport for the drive from the airport. By then, they could be too late to save anyone.

"Did you hear me, Finn? I said I'm coming for you."

"I heard you." Finn didn't want to give up, but it was hard to be positive when all hope seemed to be lost. "Hurry."

❖

Luisa heard defeat in Finn's voice. She didn't like it. She tucked her cell phone in her pocket as she boarded the transport plane, more determined than ever to bring Javier Villalobos and the rest of the Jaguars to justice.

The bad guys are not going to win today. Not on my watch.

She placed her helmet and goggles on the seat beside her and checked her gear. Gloves, body armor, pistol, battle rifle, plus a supply of tear gas canisters. Everything she needed to take on a mob—or fend off an army. In this case, an army of highly trained mercenaries fighting for their lives with little to no regard for the lives of the women they were holding against their will.

Director Chavez took the seat to her left.

"I know this mission is personal for you," he said as he eyed the sniper rifle she had added to her arsenal at the last minute. "But I need you to keep your emotions in check."

"I know, sir. You can count on me."

"Don't make me regret bringing you along, Moreno."

"I won't, sir."

Luisa made the promise, but she didn't know if she could keep it. Even as she said the words, she imagined the team taking Javier Villalobos not just down but out. If he did anything to cause Finn harm, she would put a bullet in him herself. Several, if need be.

"What's the plan?" she asked.

Director Chavez spread a map of the Mariposa Resort's grounds across his lap.

"Preliminary reports indicate the Jaguars have two layers of defenses. They've infiltrated the resort's security staff. The guards and the men they've apparently recruited from our ranks have ringed the resort, denying anyone entry or exit." He pointed to a building in the center of the map. "The women are being held here in the theater, the only space large enough to house everyone at once."

"How many guards are on them?" she asked as she surveyed the map.

Director Chavez shook his head.

"No one has been able to say for sure. At least ten. All of them heavily armed."

"So even if we pierce the outer layer of the Jaguars' defenses, they could still take out the hostages."

"If they haven't already."

"Let's think about this for a second. The organization is on the ropes. We've taken out their leader and their second-in-command is on the run. If they were going to kill the hostages, they would have done it fast while they still had a chance to get away."

"What are you thinking?" Director Chavez asked.

"I don't think Javier Villalobos is following orders. I think he's acting on his own. He wants something."

"Something like what?"

"Money, publicity, or an exchange of some kind. Something he wants for something we have. Whatever it is, he's willing to barter five hundred women's lives to get it."

"If he holds you somehow responsible for his grandmother's death, kidnapping your girlfriend could be his way of getting back at you. No matter what happens when we land, don't let him bait you into doing something you might regret. We're better than he is, Moreno. We're here to seek justice, not exact revenge."

Sometimes, Luisa thought as they continued to make their way to Cancún, justice and revenge were one and the same.

The winding road that led to the Mariposa Resort was filled with so many patrol cars and support vehicles the bus couldn't squeeze its way past them. Javier parked the damaged vehicle five hundred feet from the resort's entrance and shut off the engine. He held his gun loosely. Almost casually. As if he did this kind of thing every day. In contrast, the policemen that quickly formed a circle around the bus gripped their weapons so tight Finn was surprised the guns didn't snap in two. She could see the tension in the officers' faces and in their body language. One wrong move and the standoff could end in bloodshed.

"Here's what's going to happen."

Javier tossed his baseball cap and sunglasses aside, pulled LeeAnne from her seat, and pressed her against him to act as a human shield. Wesley, LeeAnne's partner, seemed torn between staying in her seat and climbing over it to scratch Javier's eyes out.

"We're going to exit the bus in an orderly fashion. Then you're going to walk, not run, to the resort and enter the theater.

Stay single file. Don't try to escape. If those chickenshit cops out there don't kill you by accident, I will do it on purpose."

"Javier Villalobos," a police officer said through a bullhorn, "throw your weapon out the window, put your hands on your head, and surrender."

Javier opened the window wide enough to shout his response.

"I'm coming out," he said in Spanish, "but I'm bringing everyone with me. Let us pass and no one gets hurt. Back up or this one gets it first."

LeeAnne trembled as Javier pressed the barrel of his gun to her head.

"No," Wesley pleaded. "Please don't."

"Shut up," Javier said in English, "or I'll pop you, too."

Finn gripped the seat in front of her and pulled herself to her feet. "What are you doing?" Ryan asked in a fierce whisper.

Finn resisted Ryan's efforts to pull her back into her seat. She had never considered herself a follower or a leader. She was more of an observer than anything else. Now, though, she needed to participate instead of watch. She raised her hands and stepped into the aisle.

"I'm the one you want, Javier. Take me. Let everyone else go and take me."

Javier turned his gun on her but didn't loosen his grip on LeeAnne.

"Aren't you the brave one? No wonder that fucking cop likes you so much."

He waved his gun at her, indicating he wanted her to move closer. Finn walked up the aisle on shaky legs. She didn't know what Javier had planned for her, but whatever happened, she hoped it would end quickly. He stopped her when she reached the first row of seats.

"That's close enough."

He looked her up and down, his eyes almost feral in their intensity. Then he pushed LeeAnne away from him and reached for her. "I was planning on killing you first. Now I think I might save you for last."

He held her as closely as a lover, his beard stubble scraping her cheek and his breath hot against her skin.

"Everyone out!" he yelled, then lowered his voice to a malevolent whisper. "This one's mine."

No one moved when he opened the door. They remained glued to their seats as if they thought he might rescind his offer without warning.

"Leave before I change my mind."

Finn watched as the women slowly disembarked and, once they were safely on the ground, ran into the waiting arms of the policemen. All except Ryan.

"Did you get lost on your way out?" Javier asked.

Ryan squared her shoulders. "Your men have my girl in there and I'm not going anywhere without her."

"It looks like we have another brave one on our hands."

"You're crazy, you know that?" Finn asked.

"Look who's talking," Ryan said. "I'm not the one who willingly handed herself over to a gun-wielding madman." She gave Javier a halfhearted shrug. "No offense, asshole."

"It's your funeral," he said. "You can have it wherever you want."

"That's a good start, Javier," the policeman with the bullhorn said. "Now hand over the rest."

"Negative," Javier said, switching to Spanish again. "These two are coming with me." He pressed the gun to Finn's temple and jerked his chin toward Ryan. "Move. Both of you."

Ryan climbed off the bus first. Finn followed. Unable to look down because of Javier's tight grip around her neck, she felt for the steps with her feet. She stumbled once and nearly went down, but Javier—probably less concerned with her well-being than his own safety—kept her from falling.

"Back off," Javier said to the encroaching officers when he and Finn reached the ground. "We're heading inside, and you're not going to stop us."

"Stand down," the officer in charge ordered.

"That's more like it," Javier said after the other officers dutifully backed away.

He spun Finn around and forced her to walk backward as Ryan led the way up the hill. Then he pointed to the police and news helicopters circling overhead.

"Smile for the camera."

When they neared the front of the resort, Finn saw the police standing on one side and the Jaguars on the other. The opposing forces flanked each other like fencers about to engage in a duel, though the weapons they held were much more powerful than swords. One side cheered Javier's approach while the other showered him with epithets. It remained to be seen which side would have the final say. Finn hoped, for her sake, it would be Luisa's.

Javier released his grip on her once they were inside the confines of the resort, but Finn's sense of impending doom grew the closer they came to the theater. What would they find when Javier's men opened its doors, a sea of anxious faces or a river of blood?

Two men wearing spandex tights and brightly colored masks stood guard outside the doors. Their bulging biceps were probably the only weapons they needed, but each sported a semiautomatic rifle to bolster his cause. A pile of confiscated cell phones sat at their feet.

No wonder the dozen or so calls Ryan had made to Jill on the way back from Chichén Itzá had gone directly to voice mail. Javier's men had taken everyone's phones so their owners couldn't communicate with the outside world, and powered them off so their locations couldn't be traced.

"Is everything in order?" Javier asked in Spanish.

"Yes," one of the men said.

"Show me."

The man opened one of the double doors. Finn heard several gasps of fear as hundreds of heads swiveled in their direction.

Ryan rushed inside and scanned the crowd. The room sat a little over five hundred and nearly all the seats were taken. On the far side of the room, Aurora, Sasha, Katie, and Jules sat near Jill, who thrust her arm in the air and began waving frantically.

"Here. I'm over here."

Ryan took a step toward her, then turned to make sure Javier didn't plan to shoot her in the back if she moved.

"Go," he said dismissively as he tucked his gun in his waistband.

Ryan ran across the room and into Jill's arms. Finn smiled as she watched the tear-filled reunion. Then she allowed her gaze to wander, taking in the faces of all the wonderful women she had met during the week.

"They're alive. They're all alive."

"Not for long," Javier said. "As soon as your girlfriend gets here, you're all going to die. And so is she."

❖

Luisa tried to call Finn as soon as her plane touched down in Cancún, but Finn didn't pick up. Luisa didn't want to imagine what that might mean, especially after she opened her phone's Internet browser, performed a search on the developing incident at the Mariposa, and watched news footage of Javier leading Finn and another woman inside the resort at gunpoint while dozens of law enforcement officials looked on helplessly.

"There were thirty-nine women on the bus," she said, thinking out loud. "He released all except two. Why did he let the others go?"

Director Chavez furrowed his brow as he considered the question.

"He may be trying to establish good will, which means we might be able to make a deal with him to release the rest of the hostages."

"The last time we tried to bargain with a member of the Villalobos family, the end result wasn't what we hoped."

She could still see Mrs. Villalobos tumbling out her living room window, the moment playing out in a strange combination of slow motion and high speed.

"We've got to try again," Director Chavez said. "We've got no choice."

Luisa and the rest of the members of Director Chavez's handpicked team crossed the tarmac. The ground troops climbed into the backs of two waiting vans. The snipers boarded a helicopter and waited to be deployed. Luisa didn't know which direction to turn. Should she try to find a seat in one of the armored vehicles or in the chopper?

"You're with me, Moreno," Director Chavez said.

"Yes, sir."

Luisa didn't know whether to feel disappointed or elated as the van's rear door slammed shut and the driver began heading for the Mariposa. Ground troops did most of the work during confrontations like the one they were about to have with the Jaguars, but snipers received most of the glory. In a matter of seconds, one well-placed shot could end a standoff that had endured for hours. Luisa relished the opportunity to learn at Director Chavez's side, but she wanted to be the one to end this nightmare once and for all. Not for glory or attention. She wanted to end it for Finn. Javier Villalobos had her and she meant to get her back. No matter what the cost.

She could feel everyone's excitement ratchet up a notch or two as they drew closer to the Mariposa Resort. They had trained for incidents like this time and time again, but this wasn't a glorified training session. It was very, very real. Lives were at stake. The hostages' as well as their own.

"Don't forget to breathe, Moreno," someone said. "You won't do anyone any good if you pass out."

Director Chavez laughed first and everyone else joined in, Luisa included. Even though the joke was at her expense, it had seemed lighthearted instead of malicious. She felt like she had finally earned her teammates' respect. All it had taken was finding the leader of the Jaguars, solving the mystery of Carlos Ramos's disappearance, and putting her life on the line for a rescue attempt that could very easily become a recovery mission. No biggie.

The armored vans pulled up outside the Mariposa, and everyone piled out.

"Take your positions," Director Chavez ordered.

Luisa and the other members of the team fanned out, supplementing the ranks of the weary local and state police officers who had been staring down the Jaguars' gunmen for nearly six hours.

Joint operations were normally cockfights between warring factions determined to prove whose dick was bigger. Therefore, Luisa was surprised to see the relieved look on the commander of the state troopers' face when he ceded control to Director Chavez.

"What do we have?" Director Chavez asked.

"The hotel has five hundred guests this week, but

approximately one hundred went on optional excursions today. Of that number, only two returned to the resort. We successfully diverted two busloads when we figured out what was happening. Javier Villalobos commandeered the other bus and let thirty-seven of the thirty-nine passengers go. With that said, we have, by my rough estimate, four hundred twenty to four hundred thirty guests and employees being held."

"By employees, are you referring to employees of the hotel or the tour group renting it this week?"

"By all accounts, all the hotel employees were paid handsomely not to show up today. If you see anyone in a hotel uniform, they're in on the plot. The employees I'm referring to are from SOS Tours only."

"Four hundred twenty to four hundred thirty friendlies. How many hostiles?"

"Between forty and sixty. We outnumber them, but they have the advantage. If we try to take them out by force, the hostages could get caught in the crossfire—if the Jaguars don't take them out first."

"Have you tried negotiating with them?" Luisa asked.

The commander shook his head. "They don't want to talk to me. They've been waiting for you. Why do you think I'm so glad to see you guys?"

"I thought it was my pretty face," Director Chavez said.

The commander's smile didn't reach his eyes. Director Chavez clapped him on the shoulder to boost his flagging spirits. "Good job, Hector. I'll take it from here." He turned to one of the men dressed like a security guard. "Since your boss has been waiting to talk to me, you might as well tell him I'm here."

The faux security guard with a jaguar tattoo on his left forearm eyed Director Chavez contemptuously as he gripped a Beretta in one hand and a nickel-plated Sig Sauer in the other.

"He already knows. He'll send for you when he's ready."

Director Chavez was a powerful man who possessed and wielded great authority. He obviously didn't enjoy being treated like a lowly errand boy. The muscles in his jaw crawled as he bit back his fury in order to avoid putting the upcoming negotiations at risk.

"Do you have a plan?" Luisa asked as they waited for Javier to stop playing games and get down to business.

"I have a couple things in mind, but I want to hear what he has to say before I put anything in motion. I want to end this peacefully, but if Villalobos's demands are unreasonable, he will leave me no choice but to use force."

"How do we do that without endangering the hostages?"

"That's the part I haven't worked through yet." Director Chavez rubbed his chin as he pondered the dire situation. "I want to save everyone, but we have to accept the possibility that some losses might be necessary in order to achieve our ultimate goal."

Luisa thought of the hundreds of people on both sides of the law who had already fallen victim to the Jaguars. Soldiers, rival gang members, farmers, students, and countless others who had been unfortunate enough to cross the cartel members' paths. There had already been too many losses in this war and, if she had anything to say about it, there wouldn't be any more. Not today at least.

A few minutes later, the hit man with two guns and a bad attitude tucked the Beretta in his waistband and tossed Director Chavez a cell phone.

"The boss is ready to talk to you now."

Director Chavez regarded the phone as if it might be booby-trapped. Then he turned to Luisa.

"How do I place this damned thing on speaker?"

Luisa examined the phone's display and pressed the appropriate icon.

"Director Arturo Chavez. Who am I speaking with?"

"Don't try my patience, Chavez," Javier said. "You know who this is."

"Tell me what you want, Villalobos, so the women you're holding can put this incident behind them and try to enjoy what's left of their vacations."

"Straight to the point," Javier said humorlessly. "Don't you want to get to know me better before you try to fuck me?"

Director Chavez's cheeks colored from anger, embarrassment, or both.

"My people have you and your men surrounded, Villalobos. You can't possibly escape. Your only hope of survival is me. Stop playing games and tell me what you want so everyone can walk out of here alive, including you."

Javier's laugh was as sinister as Vincent Price's during his heyday as the king of horror. Filtered through the cheap throwaway phone's crackly speaker, the sound sent chills down Luisa's spine.

"You want to know what I want?" Javier said. "Okay, I'll tell you. I want one hundred million dollars in cash and safe passage for me and my men."

"Let's be clear. If I get you what you want, you will release the hostages unharmed?"

"Cross my heart and hope to die. On second thought, I'd better not say that too loud. Your men are probably listening and they're itching to kill me. Unlike my grandmother, I'm not going to take the easy way out. And I may take a few of your men with me just for fun."

Director Chavez patted the air with his free hand, trying to control someone he couldn't see.

"What happened with your grandmother was tragic, I admit, but the outcome was her decision. You can make a different choice, Javier. A smarter choice."

"My grandmother was the most brilliant person I've ever met in my life," Javier said, anger creeping into his voice. "She taught me everything I know. Now I have to learn from her mistake."

"What mistake might that be?" Director Chavez asked cautiously.

"She should have killed that bitch Luisa Moreno the first chance she got instead of giving Moreno time to dig up the dirt on us and our organization. If she had, you and I wouldn't be having this tedious conversation right now. You know what? I've changed my mind. Besides the money and the free ride, there's one more thing you can get me."

"What do you want?"

Luisa knew what Javier was going to say even before the words left his mouth.

"I want Luisa Moreno."

❖

Javier's men had ordered everyone to be quiet, but Finn heard women whispering all around her. She tried to block out the words of comfort, the guilt-ridden apologies for past slights, and the promises of what everyone would do if they were fortunate enough to get out of here alive as she strained to hear Javier's half of his animated telephone conversation. She had missed the first part of the call because he was out of earshot. Once he moved closer, she tried desperately to bring herself up to speed.

Javier's lack of deference meant he probably wasn't talking to his boss, but she could tell by his demeanor he was talking to someone important. Someone who might be able to save their lives.

"I knew I should have studied Spanish instead of French in high school," Ryan said. "I can't understand a damned thing he's saying. What's he going on about? Who is he talking to?"

"I'm not sure yet."

Enough time had passed for the Federal Police to travel from Mexico City. If Luisa and her cohorts had arrived, Finn and her fellow guests' collective nightmare might be about to come to an end. Or perhaps it was just beginning. Because if the police were here, now the real drama was about to begin.

"He must be talking with the *Federales*," she said. "The legitimate ones, not the corrupt ones he's paying to be on his side. I think he just gave his list of demands."

"What does he want?" Jill asked.

"One hundred million dollars and safe passage for him and his men."

Aurora blew out a disgusted sigh.

"A hundred-million-dollar payoff? That's never going to happen."

"Why do you say that?" Finn asked. She knew the American government had a long-standing policy about refusing to negotiate with terrorists. Did the Mexican government have a similar rule? If so, did this situation apply?

"There's no way in hell the Mexican government will pay these bastards that kind of money and let them walk out of here scot-free," Aurora said. "Not with everyone watching. These guys might have been able to get away with holding us captive if there weren't news helicopters circling overhead and a beach full of curious spectators watching this spectacle play out. After those forty-three students were found burned alive, neither the government nor the tourist industry can afford another scandal. The president might have felt pressured to pay up just to keep things quiet. But it's too late for that now. This scandal has already broken. Neither side wants to come out on the losing end, but I don't see them meeting halfway. The government can't make any concessions or they'll look soft. And these guys aren't going to back down because they have nothing to lose. If anything, they're going to dig in even harder."

"Where does that leave us?" Jill asked.

"Exactly where we are now." Ryan glanced at the gunmen ringing the room, one every few feet and two in front of each exit. "Caught in the middle."

"Shh." Finn hoped she had translated Javier's last sentence correctly. "I think he just said he's changed his mind."

"Yeah? Is he letting us go?" Finn's expression caused the hope in Jill's voice to fade before it could take root. "What does he want?"

"Not what," Finn said disconsolately. "Who. He wants Luisa."

"The cop you're seeing?" Ryan asked. "Why does he want her?"

Finn could think of only two possible scenarios, neither very desirable. "Either he wants to kill her or he wants her to watch me die."

"We can't just sit here," Ryan said. "We've got to do something. It's just like on the bus. There are more of them now, but the numbers are still on our side."

"Unless you've got a stash of C4 in your pocket, the firepower's still on theirs."

"I don't care. The next time they let us out to use the bathroom, I'm making a run for it."

"If you manage to get away, what do you think will happen to the ones you leave behind?" Aurora asked. "The ones who can't run."

Ryan's cheeks colored as she regarded Aurora's wheelchair. "I'm sorry, but I'm tired of sitting around waiting for someone to rescue us. Maybe it's time we saved ourselves."

"I hear you," Finn said, "but we're in over our heads with this one. We might have had an outside chance of success on the bus, but we have zero chance here at the resort. Even if we managed to fight our way past the guys in here, there are more waiting outside. I know it's frustrating, but we need to leave it to the professionals this time. It might take a while, but I know they can come up with a way to get us out of this."

"How can you be so certain?" Ryan asked. "You saw how badly the state police bungled the attempted rescue when we were on the bus. Instead of saving us, they put us and themselves in even more danger. Based on that sad performance, do you really have that much faith the Federal Police can do much better?"

"No," Finn was forced to admit, "but I have faith in Luisa Moreno, and that's all that counts."

❖

Luisa put down her guns and began stripping off her protective gear.

Director Chavez placed his hand over the cell phone's speaker.

"What the hell do you think you're doing, Moreno?"

"I'm trying to save the hostages. Villalobos asked for me. I'm turning myself over to him."

"What are you trying to do, get yourself killed? Put your vest back on. I'm not letting you anywhere near that guy. Let me keep trying to negotiate with him first. The initial demand is rarely if ever the final one. If we agree to fulfill his request too soon, he'll think we're weak and he'll ask for more, not less. I need him to show us a sign of good faith before I even think of giving him anything. And there's no way in the world I'm letting him walk out of here with a single peso, let alone one hundred million dollars and one of my best officers to boot. Understood?"

"Yes, sir."

Director Chavez looked at her to make sure they were on the same page, then nodded and returned to his call.

"All right, Villalobos. Let me get this straight. You want money, transportation, and Officer Moreno. If I give you these things, what do I get in return?"

"You get to walk away with your reputation intact," Javier said. "I'm offering you a chance to be a hero or a scapegoat. You can be the man who saved four hundred thirty hostages or the man responsible for getting them all killed. It's your choice. What will it be? Are you going to give me what I want, or are you going to keep wasting my time?"

"It's after seven. The banks are closed at this time of day. Even if one were still open, it would take several hours to put that kind of ransom together. One hundred million dollars is a lot of money."

"You don't need to go to a bank when you have piles of cash sitting in evidence rooms all around the country. You have at least five million dollars of our money, in addition to the assets you've seized from other cartels. Unless the president has spent it all paying for that cushy property in the Lomas district his soap star wife got on credit from a government contractor, your people are sitting on a hell of a lot more money than I've asked for. You have one hour to give me my share."

"One hour isn't enough time."

"One hour, Chavez, or I start shooting hostages. One will die every fifteen minutes until I get what I want. Don't make me wait too long or the price will double. So will the body count."

"Be reasonable, Javier. I'm trying to negotiate in good faith. Give me the courtesy of doing the same. One hour isn't long enough and you know it. You've got to give me some leeway."

"How much time do you need?"

Javier's world-weary sigh made him sound even more like a petulant child than his exorbitant demand.

"At least twelve hours," Director Chavez said. "Maybe more. The amount of money you're demanding is above my pay grade. I need time to get clearance from my superiors. If they approve, then I'll need time to locate the money and arrange transportation for you and your men."

"You have six hours, not a second more. And don't forget about the most important part of my request."

Director Chavez eyed Luisa. "I can get you the money, and I can round up enough vehicles to get you and your men safe passage out of here, but there's nothing you could say to convince me to hand over Officer Moreno to you."

"You know what they say. Actions speak louder than words. And I think it's time I showed you that your actions have consequences if you cross me."

"Villalobos, wait," Director Chavez pleaded, but the line had gone dead.

A few seconds later, Luisa heard screams from inside the theater. Then the double doors on the right side of the building opened and Javier walked out with a weeping woman in tow. The woman had short hair and broad shoulders. She was wearing sandals, board shorts, and a loose-fitting tank top over a black sports bra. A silver ball and chain necklace dangled between her breasts. She looked ready for a day at the beach or a night by the pool. Instead, Javier forced her to her knees and placed the barrel of his gun to the back of her head.

Luisa raised her AR-15 and set her sights on Javier. She flexed her finger against the trigger but didn't squeeze. She had the shot. The one she had been waiting for her entire career. With one bullet, she could put an end to Javier Villalobos, but at what cost? He was only one man. Even if she killed him, there were sixty more just like him standing between her and Finn. And countless more under his command. Killing him wasn't enough. But it was a damn good start.

"Stand down, Moreno," Director Chavez ordered. He turned to the rest of his troops. "That goes for you, too. Lower your weapons. All of you."

Luisa and her colleagues reluctantly complied, but it didn't stop Javier from pulling the trigger. The woman's lifeless body pitched forward as she fell facedown on the sidewalk.

Javier looked up. His words were aimed at Director Chavez, but his gaze was focused on Luisa.

"You've got six hours. See you then."

❖

Finn pulled Katie into her arms and tried to assuage her grief over Sasha, but she could barely control her own fear. She could still see the panicked look in Sasha's eyes and the stricken expression on her face when Javier pulled her from her seat and marched her outside. She could still hear the gunshot that had taken Sasha's life—and Katie's heartfelt wail for her lost friend. Sasha's death had obviously been meant as a warning. Would it force the Federal Police to give in to Javier's demands, or compel them to stand their ground?

"Do you still want to sit around and do nothing?" Ryan asked. "Any one of us could be next."

"I think we should wait for the deadline to pass," Jill said. "If he gets the money he asked for, he might let us go."

"How can he?" Ryan asked. "Whether he gets the money or not, we're witnesses. All of us have seen his face. So has everyone outside. He executed Sasha right in front of them."

Finn pressed a hand over Katie's ear as fresh sobs racked her body. Ryan's voice softened.

"He doesn't intend to let us go. If he doesn't get the money, he's going to kill someone else. And he'll keep killing until he runs out of victims, the Federal Police give in to his demands, or someone grows some balls and takes him out. And if he does get the money, he'll probably use some of us as human security blankets to escort him to safety while his men use the rest for target practice. We're dead either way."

"What's your plan?" Finn asked.

Ryan shrugged. "I don't have one yet, but we have six hours to figure something out. Otherwise, these guys will start picking us off one by one. I don't know about you, but I would rather die on my own terms than someone else's."

A few hours ago, Finn had offered to sacrifice her life for thirty-eight others'. She wondered if Javier would be willing to make a similar trade now.

"It's me he wants."

"Not anymore. He was using you and the rest of us as bait to get the Federal Police here. He wants Luisa, not you. I don't even think he wants the money. If he did, he wouldn't have asked for nearly as much. He just wants her. I don't know what she did to piss him off, but he obviously wants to get back at her for something. This whole thing is about revenge. We have six hours to deny him his and exact our own. For Sasha. Who's with me?"

Katie lifted her head from Finn's chest and dried her eyes. "I am," she said shakily.

After everyone else in their group pledged to mount as much resistance as they could, Finn saw them turn to her. She had traveled the world alone for years now, but this next journey was one she couldn't take on her own.

"Count me in."

"Excellent," Ryan said. "Now what will we do for weapons?"

"We already have them. We just have to figure out how to use them."

Finn pointed to the dog tag around her neck and the plastic band around her wrist. A few days ago—though it felt like a lifetime now—Verity had joked about accidentally slicing off a nipple in the shower. The wristbands weren't that sharp. If used appropriately, they might be able to inflict enough damage to slow someone down but not stop them completely. With precious few resources at their disposal, they would have to take what they could get.

"All we need now is a distraction," Ryan said.

Aurora raised her hand. "Leave that part to me."

❖

Luisa removed her helmet as she watched two state troopers zip the dead woman's remains into a body bag and place them in the back of a police van.

Director Chavez looked up at the news helicopters circling overhead, then lowered his gaze to the ground.

"I should have let you take the shot."

"I'm glad you didn't. If you had, we would have more than one victim on our hands."

"We still might. The clock is ticking. Six hours isn't much time to plan our strategy."

Luisa put her helmet back on and lowered her protective visor into place. "Would you like me to get the president on the line?"

"No, he would be a fool to authorize that kind of payout and I would be an even bigger fool to ask him to do it. Let's not drag this out any longer than we need to. This ends tonight. And it ends with us."

"What do you want me to do?"

Director Chavez handed her a tablet computer. "I need you to find me something that shows the electric plan for the entire resort and someone who knows how to access it. Villalobos and his men have enough food and water available to them to hole up indefinitely. If we don't take them out of their comfort zone, they could dig in for weeks. First, we'll cut the air-conditioning. I want them to sweat. Literally and figuratively. If we do it remotely, Villalobos won't be able to pin the blame on us. The sun is setting, but it's still pretty hot out here. Inside, the conditions will become oppressive in no time at all. We can send one of our guys in disguised as an electrician. Once he gains access to the control panel, he can install a camera that will allow us to see what's going on in that room. When the right moment presents itself, we'll cut the lights and put them in the dark. While they're feeling their way around, we'll drop a team of snipers on the roof and use our night vision goggles to attack them from the air and on the ground."

Luisa thought the plan sounded strong though not foolproof. "Even if I find the information we're looking for," she said, "we'll still need someone to give us the access codes."

"The hotel's assistant manager is on his way now," Hector Salinas said. "He saw the coverage on TV and called in to offer his help."

"Have you vetted him?" Director Chavez asked.

"Yes, he's on our side."

"It's a risky plan," Luisa said as she paged through screens on the tablet.

"I know," Director Chavez said. "And there's a chance we might end up with casualties on all fronts, but the scheme has to work because I don't have a Plan B. Not one I'm willing to employ, anyway." He looked at her out of the corner of his eye. "Were you willing to sacrifice yourself in order to save one woman or four hundred?"

"Does it matter?"

"Yes, it does. I included you on this mission because you promised not to let your emotions get the better of you."

"And I won't."

Director Chavez's jaw tightened. He looked like he wanted to believe her but thought she wasn't being entirely truthful.

"We're responsible for every woman in there," he reminded her, "not just one."

"I realize that, sir. And I intend to save as many as I can."

But her mission would feel like a failure if Finn wasn't one of them.

❖

The room was starting to feel like an oven. At first, Finn thought the collected body heat was to blame. Then she realized the temperature had been cooler before the sun set than after.

"Is it hot in here," she said as she fanned herself with her shirt to get more air, "or is it just me?"

"When was the last time the AC kicked on?" Ryan asked, but no one could come up with the answer.

"Do you think it's intentional?" Jill asked, nearly mouthing the words.

Finn thought it over. "It might be. I wish I knew what the Federal Police were planning so we could synchronize our actions with theirs. I don't want to make a move if they have something better in mind."

"If they did," Ryan said, "they would have put it to use by now."

Finn sighed in frustration. She hated not knowing what was going on outside the resort, but she hated the loss of control even more. No matter what exotic locale or unusual circumstance in which she found herself in the past, she had always been free to make her own decisions. She had always been in control of her own life. Until now. This experience was a first for her. And one she would rather not repeat. But this experience had also allowed her to meet Luisa. That was ample reason to do it all over again.

"How long do you want to wait?" Katie asked.

Finn looked at her watch. Two hours had passed since Javier issued his ultimatum, which meant the Federal Police had four hours left to grant his request or he would randomly execute someone else. Should they try to save themselves now or wait for the Federal Police to rescue them? She told herself to be smart. Doing something rash might get someone killed. But so could doing nothing at all, if Sasha's senseless death was any example.

"There's no time like the present," Ryan said. "Is everyone ready?"

Everyone nodded. Everyone except Aurora. She had offered to provide a distraction, but Finn didn't think her present condition was part of the ruse. Her face was ashen and her clothes were soaked with perspiration.

"Aurora, are you all right?"

Finn touched Aurora's arm. Her skin, normally so warm, was clammy and cool.

"I'm fine," Aurora said, though she looked and sounded far from it.

Her voice was weak and her chest heaved as if she had just finished a marathon. Her pulse raced beneath Finn's fingers.

"No, you're not. I think you need a doctor."

Aurora tried to downplay Finn's concerns.

"I just got a little overheated. I'll be fine as soon as the air comes back on."

But the air conditioner still wasn't running and the temperature in the room continued to climb.

"We can use this," Ryan said under her breath.

Finn took another look at Aurora, who seemed to be growing weaker by the second. Her eyelids were at half-mast and her head bobbed as if she might be losing consciousness.

"Whatever you have in mind, do it. And do it fast."

Ryan nodded and pushed herself to her feet.

"What are you trying to do," she asked as the gunmen turned their weapons in her direction, "roast us to death?"

"Sit down and shut up."

Javier paced the front of the room, his agitation growing each time the reading on the thermostat kicked up another degree.

"But this woman is in distress," Ryan said. "She needs help."

"Don't make me come up there for nothing. Because if I find out you're lying and she's faking, I will kill both of you."

Jill joined in. "Look at her. Does it look like she's faking? She's about to pass out. So are the rest of us."

Dozens of women murmured in agreement. Everyone was suffering, but Aurora seemed to be affected by the oppressive heat the most.

"If you don't do something," Finn said, "you're going to have another death on your hands."

Javier waved one of his men over. Finn could see Ryan itching to try to overpower the man and take his gun, but two more of Javier's henchmen held her and Jill at bay. The man placed the back of his hand on Aurora's forehead, then pried her fluttering eyelids open with his thumbs. After he completed his amateur examination, he shook his head and backed away.

"So she is faking her 'condition'?" Javier asked with a smirk.

"No, boss." The man crossed himself and kissed the crucifix hanging around his neck. "I think she's dying."

"I pay you to follow orders," Javier said. "I don't pay you to think."

Aurora didn't look good, true enough, but Finn didn't think she was as bad off as the man was making her out to be. Yet.

"Out of the way."

Javier brushed past his men and adjusted the thermostat on the air conditioner. When the unit didn't kick on, he cursed in Spanish, then slapped his hands against the wall and came over to take a look at Aurora himself.

"Now are you going to get her the help she needs?" Finn asked.

"She doesn't need help. What she needs is to be put out of her misery."

"But you won't hurt her."

"What?"

Finn sensed confusion in him. Confusion and uncertainty. When he looked at her, she saw the eyes of a scared little boy instead of a hardened killer. He looked like someone used to taking orders, not giving them. Now he was on his own. There was no one left to tell him what to do.

"Let her go. Let *us* go. It's what your grandmother would want you to do."

He snorted. “My grandmother is the reason we’re here.”

“But you’re in charge now. You can end this.”

His expression hardened. “I intend to. My way.” He grabbed Aurora’s chair and began to wheel her down the aisle.

“Where are you taking her?” Finn took a step toward him, but one of the gunmen shoved her back in her seat.

“You asked for my help, didn’t you?” Javier said. “I’m giving it to you. But I want something in return.”

When he reached for his cell phone, Finn wondered how high a price they would have to pay.

❖

Luisa was getting anxious. Based on the conversation she had just overheard between Director Chavez and President Enrique Peña Nieto, so was the government.

While the president didn’t want to pay the outrageous ransom Javier Villalobos had requested, he also didn’t want any repeats of the tragic scene that had played out on televisions across the country a few hours ago when Villalobos executed a hostage in full view of the news helicopters circling overhead. But, tellingly, he didn’t offer any advice on how to get the job done.

The president and the rest of his cabinet were already facing serious criticism for their actions following the disappearance and subsequent murder of nearly fifty first-year students enrolled in Ayotzinapa Rural Teachers College. On September 26, 2013, the students were ordered by a radical leftist group associated with their school to disrupt a party planned by María de los Ángeles Pineda, the wife of the mayor of Iguala, a small town in Guerrero. Mayor José Luis Abarca ordered local police to stop the students, who were traveling in stolen buses. After their motorcade was intercepted, the students threw rocks at the police, who responded with gunfire. Three students were killed on the spot. The rest were taken away and turned over to the members of a local drug cartel called United Warriors, who killed them and burned their bodies. The federal government claimed Mayor Abarca and his wife had ties to the United Warriors.

Though the government's claims seemed to be legitimate, it didn't help its cause during the search for the Ayotzinapa students when investigators uncovered several clandestine burial sites in Guerrero, announced the remains were those of the missing students, and were then proven wrong. The public was horrified, and the government was left with a public relations disaster, which only grew worse after the attorney general solved the case in record time, a rarity in a country where ninety-eight percent of murders went unsolved each year. More than seventy people were detained, including Mayor Abarca and his wife. Several people confessed to kidnapping and executing the students, but citizens launched protests and began demanding President Peña Nieto's resignation. The protest leaders said the incident was a state crime and, as a result, the head of the Mexican state needed to resign.

President Peña Nieto defiantly refused to resign and promised to serve the rest of his six-year term, but the government was understandably afraid to use force against the demonstrators as they blockaded roads, stole vehicles, looted supermarkets, and set fire to government buildings. Would Luisa and her colleagues be forced to stand idly by while the Jaguars thumbed their noses at them, too?

"The president wants results, but how are we supposed to get them when we're standing around with our dicks in our hands? Present company excepted." Despite the tense situation, Director Chavez managed a smile as he reversed course. "Then again, you have a bigger pair of balls than some men I've commanded over the years. I could use more officers like you."

"Is that why you wouldn't let me go inside when Villalobos asked for me?"

"I talked you out of committing suicide. I wouldn't let you on the street when you first got here because I said you needed to prove yourself to your fellow officers."

"I've done that."

"I know. You needed to prove yourself to them, but you never needed to prove yourself to me." He placed a hand on her shoulder. "I've believed in you from the moment your application came across my desk. I can tell you've got what it takes to be a great officer, but you need to learn one thing in particular in order to reach your potential."

"What's that?" she asked, genuinely curious.

"Restraint."

Luisa had heard similar arguments from her parents over the years each time she attacked a problem head-on without thinking it through first. She had learned to take a more cerebral approach to problem solving, except when the issue at hand involved something she was especially passionate about. And she was definitely passionate about Finn Chamberlain, a woman who was a stranger six days ago but had started to feel like someone she couldn't bear to live without.

"Think before you act, Moreno. It's the most important lesson I could ever hope to teach you."

When the cell phone in Director Chavez's hand rang for the second time, Luisa knew she was about to learn the lesson firsthand.

"It's him." Director Chavez took a moment to compose himself before he answered the phone. "What's going on,

Javier? You said I had six hours to respond to your demand. The time isn't up yet."

"That's not why I'm calling. The air conditioner stopped working. But I'm sure you knew that, didn't you?"

"How would I know that? You're behind closed doors, remember? I can't get to you from here."

"If I find out you had something to do with it, Chavez, I'm going to make you regret it, understand?"

Director Chavez nodded as if Villalobos could see him. "You're calling the shots, Javier. I understand that. What do you want me to do?"

"Send someone in to fix the air conditioning. And don't try anything funny or I'll kill another hostage. I've done it before. Do you want to see me do it again?"

"No," Director Chavez said quickly. "But let's be reasonable. If I do something for you, I need you to do something for me."

"I figured you'd say that. Once the air conditioner's fixed, I'll release one of the hostages. She's more trouble than she's worth, anyway. Do we have a deal?"

"Yes. I'll get on the phone and find someone who can help. Someone should be here in less than thirty minutes."

"Make it fifteen or the deal's off."

"Whatever you say." Director Chavez ended the call and used his own phone to call David Menendez, the officer he had assigned to venture inside.

David had worn a mask over his face when he had assumed his position outside the resort so Villalobos's men weren't able to see his face. After the resort's assistant manager arrived and they were able to access the electric plan, Director Chavez had pulled David from his position and sent him into town to wait for his call.

When David arrived a few minutes after Director Chavez

summoned him, he was driving a pickup truck emblazoned with the name of a local electrician's shop. He emerged carrying a battered metal toolbox and wearing a polo shirt, jeans, and work boots. He jogged up the road, not making eye contact with any of his fellow officers or their antagonists. As soon as he got the hidden camera installed and the feed went online, Luisa would remotely restore the air conditioner to working order. David would get the credit—if he made his efforts look real. Otherwise, their deception would be discovered and David could either become another hostage or yet another of Javier's victims.

"The electrician's here," Director Chavez told Javier when he got him back on the phone. "Do you want me to send him in?"

"Not yet. I want one of my men to search him first to make sure he isn't carrying any concealed weapons."

Director Chavez relayed the order to the surly hit man who had tossed him the cell phone he was now holding. The man patted Menendez down and rummaged through his toolbox. Luisa stiffened when she saw the hit man pick up the "replacement part" containing the hidden camera. Then he casually tossed it aside, slammed the toolbox shut, and leaned toward the phone in Director Chavez's outstretched hand.

"He's clean, boss."

"Then bring him in here."

"Move."

The hit man pressed his pistols into the small of David's back and marched him toward the theater. Luisa watched until they disappeared inside. She braced herself to hear gunshots or to see the relieved face of someone unexpectedly tasting freedom after spending most of the afternoon coming to terms with her impending death. She knew she shouldn't expect the face to be Finn's, but her heart held out hope. As she tightened her grip on her battle rifle, she prayed her heart wasn't about to be broken.

"When will you release the hostage?" Director Chavez asked.

"When I see if this guy is really who he says he is," Javier said. "When will I get my money?"

"The van's on the way from Mexico City now. It should be here in about four hours."

Director Chavez hesitated long enough for Luisa to notice, but she didn't think the brief pause captured Villalobos's attention. President Peña Nieto had refused to authorize payment of the ransom. Not only the full amount, but any amount at all. Director Chavez knew Villalobos wouldn't take the news well, so he decided to string him along as long as he could while he tried to think of a way to resolve the situation while leaving the least amount of casualties behind.

"You're cutting it close, aren't you?" Javier asked.

"Like I said, these things take time."

"Just make sure yours doesn't run out. And if Luisa Moreno's with you, tell her I'm looking forward to our date."

So am I, Luisa thought, though I doubt you'll enjoy it as much as I will.

❖

Finn tensed when the electrician was shoved into the room. She couldn't help but wonder what would happen to him if he wasn't able to fix the problem. Would he be executed, too? And if he was able to do his job, would he be allowed to leave, or would he be forced to join them?

"What's your name?" Javier asked.

Obviously nervous, the electrician swallowed hard. His Adam's apple bobbed like a fishing lure caught in the currents of a rushing stream.

"David, sir. David Menendez."

"Let me tell you a secret, David. I can smell a cop from ten miles away. Did you know that?"

"No, sir."

"It's a hidden talent of mine." Javier sniffed the air. "Do you know what you smell like, David?"

Too frightened to speak, David shook his head.

"You smell like a coward. Are you a coward, David?"

"I—I don't know, sir."

"You don't know?" Javier turned to his men like a schoolyard bully seeking validation from his lackeys. "What *do* you know?"

Even from twenty feet away, Finn could see David's eyes fill with tears.

"That I don't want to die."

Javier tapped the barrel of his gun against the side of David's head.

"Then do your job. It feels like a fucking sauna in here."

"Yes, sir." David swiped his hand across his eyes. "I need to check the main unit first to see if there are any issues with it. If there aren't, I'll need to take a look at the control panel."

Javier waved him away as if he had grown bored with the conversation. "Go with him, Manuel."

David was ushered out by the same man who had brought him inside. Finn hoped the problem would be an easy fix and the air would magically start working again, but David returned several minutes later looking just as lost as he had when he had first arrived. He headed to the control panel, unscrewed the cover, and took a look at the wiring. Then he pulled something from his toolbox, inserted it into the panel, and replaced the cover. He flipped the On/Off switch a couple of times, then stepped back like he was waiting for something to happen.

Finn sighed with relief when she heard the familiar click of the air conditioner powering on and felt a blast of artificially cooled air from the vent overhead hit her in the face.

David packed his toolbox and hesitantly approached Javier. “May I leave now?”

“Go.” Javier jerked his chin in Aurora’s direction. “And take her with you.”

David fiddled with the controls on Aurora’s wheelchair until he got it going in the right direction. Then he practically ran out of the room, Manuel hot on his heels. Finn wished everyone else could follow in their wake.

Their ordeal was supposed to end in a few hours, but she sensed it had barely begun.

❖

“Here they come.”

Luisa lowered the tablet computer when she saw David and one of the hostages exit the theater with one of Javier’s hit men trailing them. The hostage was slumped over in her motorized wheelchair. David wrapped an arm around her shoulders to keep her from falling as they slowly made their way over the bumpy terrain.

“Is she alive?” Director Chavez asked.

“Yes,” David said. “She was overcome by the heat, but I think she’ll be fine.”

Director Chavez eyed the hit man as he backed away, each waiting for the other to make a move.

"Drive her to the nearest hospital and get her checked out. Sanchez, Avila. Help him get her loaded in the truck."

Two officers stepped forward and followed David to the borrowed truck. They lifted the hostage from her wheelchair and placed her in the front seat. After they loaded the wheelchair in the back of the truck, David drove away, and Sanchez and Avila returned to their positions.

"What do we have?" Director Chavez asked.

Luisa returned her attention to the camera feed displayed on the computer. Using the icons on the touch screen, she turned the camera in a slow pan of the room.

"The situation's not as bad as we thought. There are more men outside than there are inside. Not including Villalobos, the hostages are being guarded by twenty men. Once we pierce the outer perimeter, the inner ring is sure to fall."

She left the rest unsaid, however. If they didn't get to the men in the inner circle fast enough, there was no telling how much damage the gunmen could inflict before they were taken down.

She panned the camera again, then zoomed in on a familiar face. Finn looked weary, but she seemed to be holding up okay. Luisa hadn't expected any less. If Finn was brave enough to travel the world alone, she was brave enough to handle anything Javier Villalobos could dish out. For Finn's sake, Luisa hoped the worst was already behind her, but she feared the worst was yet to come.

She didn't know Villalobos's end game, but she knew he wasn't going to give up without a fight. And neither was she.

"We need to put our heads together," Director Chavez said.

He used his cell phone to call the various squadron leaders under his command since radio communications were limited to coded, mission-specific exchanges in case the compromised officers on Villalobos's side were tuned to the same frequency. When the men arrived, everyone huddled over the tablet computer while Director Chavez planned the rescue mission that would mark the Federal Police's finest hour—or one of its most devastating defeats.

"Does everyone understand their roles?" Director Chavez asked.

Everyone responded in the affirmative.

"Good. Resume your positions and make sure the rest of the team is in the loop as well. We move on my signal. Understood?"

"Yes, sir."

"What would you like me and my men to do?" Hector Salinas asked.

"Get these vehicles out of here. We need to get this driveway cleared as soon as possible."

"You got it, Arturo."

Director Chavez's cell phone rang shortly after Salinas and his men began the laborious process of moving the dozens of cars parked haphazardly all along the winding driveway. The director nodded as if he had been expecting the call.

"What's going on out there, Chavez?" Javier asked. "My men are telling me you're up to something."

"I'm not up to anything. I'm simply fulfilling the terms of our agreement. Three vans are on the way. One contains the cash you requested, the other two will be used to provide safe passage for you and your men. If you want your money and a way out, I need to make room for the vehicles that can give you both."

"What about the other thing I asked for? What about Luisa Moreno?"

Director Chavez met Luisa's eye and held her gaze.

"I'll hand her over to you after you release the hostages, not before."

His voice sounded sincere, but his expression said he had no intention of keeping his word.

"If you think I'm giving up all my leverage, you're crazy. After I get Moreno and the money, *then* you get the hostages."

"Now you're asking me to give up my leverage. If this is going to work, you have to at least meet me halfway. I give you the money, you release the hostages, then I give you Moreno. That's the best I can do."

"I'm done making deals, Chavez."

Villalobos sounded increasingly agitated. Luisa feared he was dangerously close to becoming completely unhinged, which could put the hostages in even more peril than they already were.

"Now get me what I asked for or you get nothing."

Nothing was what Villalobos and his men had to lose. For the moment, Luisa and her colleagues still had everything to gain. Time would tell which side would win. And time, Luisa knew, was running out. Director Chavez had preached patience and restraint. But if they waited much longer, their patience could become a liability instead of a virtue.

Director Chavez's personal cell phone rang. He handed it to Luisa while he continued trying to bargain with Javier Villalobos.

"The director is busy at the moment," she said, feeling more like a secretary than a federal officer. "This is Luisa Moreno. How may I help you?"

"Moreno, it's me, David Menendez. I'm calling from the hospital. The hostage Villalobos released has regained consciousness and is starting to talk."

"Has she given you any information we can use?"

"She says the rest of the hostages are getting anxious. They're planning some kind of attack. As soon as they see an opening, they're going to turn on their captors."

On the tablet's screen, Luisa could see Finn and the women sitting near her watching the gunmen holding them as if they were waiting to spring into action. What were they thinking? They had the superior numbers, but they were hopelessly outgunned.

"What are they going to fight with, their bare hands? They're unarmed and untrained. I admire their bravery, but if they make a move on Villalobos and his men, it would not only be futile but suicidal."

"I agree, but if you were in their position, would you wait for someone else to decide your fate, or would you take matters into your own hands? You would fight. So would I. You can't hold it against them for doing something you would do yourself."

"I don't, but based on what you just told me, our mission has changed. We not only have to save the hostages from Villalobos, we need to save them from themselves. The way things are going, I don't know if we'll be able to do either."

She felt like pulling her hair out. She knew the mission's failure would haunt her for more than the rest of her career. It would haunt her for the rest of her life.

"Talk to me, Moreno," Director Chavez said after he was unable to convince Villalobos to modify his demands. "What did Menendez have to say?"

Luisa filled him in on what Menendez had told her about the hostages' plan to revolt.

"We've got to move in, sir, and we've got to do it now."

Director Chavez nodded soberly as if the matter was settled, but Luisa wasn't done.

"You need to let me go inside, sir. Handing me over gives

us our best chance to beat this guy. You know it as well as I do."

As Director Chavez eyed the news helicopters circling overhead and the onlookers crowding the beach, Luisa could see the indecision etched on his face. She could practically read his thoughts. Was he doing the right thing? Had he waited too long to make his move, or was he about to act too soon?

He reached for his cell phone after the first of two armored vans pulled into the resort's winding driveway.

"You win, Javier."

Luisa's adrenaline spiked. One way or another, the standoff was about to come to an end—and whether she wanted it or not, she would have a front row seat.

"Moreno's coming in."

Day Seven

Finn glanced at her watch as the display changed from p.m. to a.m. A new day had arrived. This was supposed to be the beginning of her last full day at the Mariposa Resort. Now it could turn out to be her last day on earth.

She had always wondered how she would spend her last moments. When the time came, would she find herself alone in a far-flung locale or would she be surrounded by family and friends in the cozy confines of home? This scenario had never occurred to her. Surrounded by hundreds of women who were strangers less than a week ago but now felt like family.

She looked around the room. It had been more than twelve hours since Javier's men had invaded the resort. Many of the hostages were starting to flag. Finn saw exhaustion and despair etched on their faces. The men holding them were undoubtedly tired, too, but their eyes glittered with what looked like anticipation. If the Mexican government met their demands, in less than an hour, they could all be very rich men. And everyone else in the room would either be free or dead.

Nervous tension turned the muscles in Finn's neck, back, and shoulders into knots. She craned her neck to ease the pain, then placed her hands on her knees to stop her legs from shaking. She had experienced many things during her travels—

from flight delays to lost luggage to lousy accommodations to natural disasters—but she had never experienced anything like this. The complete and utter certainty that she and everyone with her was about to die.

"Are you having second thoughts?" Ryan asked. "If you are, you aren't the only one." She took Jill's hand and held it in both of hers. "Maybe you were right. Maybe we should wait and see what the *Federales* have in mind."

Earlier, Ryan had been gung ho about going after Javier and his men. She seemed considerably less enthusiastic now that she had something—*someone*—to lose. She and Jill had been glued to each other ever since they were reunited. If they were fortunate enough to make it home, Finn thought they would remain that way for years to come. Seeing their connection made her miss the one she had started to establish with Luisa. And it made her wonder if she and Luisa would have a chance to explore their burgeoning relationship instead of watching it wither and perish before it had a chance to reach full bloom.

This week had felt like the start of something. Today could be the end. Of everything that was. And everything that was yet to be.

She had spent most of her childhood feeling rejected. Feeling broken. Feeling like no one would ever want to be involved with someone like her. Someone who was different from everyone she knew in almost every way. A brainiac amongst the jocks. A lesbian in a sea of heterosexuals. A stutterer surrounded by people who had no problems speaking freely—especially when they were hurling insults in her direction.

She had gotten used to being alone. Along the way, she had managed to convince herself that she liked it. Lasting connections, she told herself, were something to be avoided rather than pursued. Then a tall, dark stranger sat next to her in an airport bar and everything had begun to change. She had been drawn to Luisa, intrigued by her. In a matter of hours, she had fallen into bed with her. In a matter of days, she had fallen in love with her. Then the words had come tumbling out. The words she had never thought she would say. The words she might not get a chance to say again.

I love you, Luisa, she thought. Come for me.

When the double doors near the front of the room swung open, she instantly regretted her silent plea.

Luisa walked into the theater with her arms outstretched and her gloved hands facing the ceiling. The pose made her look more than a little like the bird girl statue on the cover of the infamous tell-all that had made Savannah, Georgia, even more of a tourist mecca than it already was prior to the book's publication. She was in full uniform. In spite of the helmet on her head, the bulky bulletproof vest protecting her upper body, and the knee pads with a hard exoskeleton strapped around her legs, she looked vulnerable. Defenseless.

"Is that your girl?" Ryan asked. "The cop you were talking to on the bus?"

Finn nodded.

"What is she doing here?" Jill asked.

"What she does best: putting herself at risk in order to save someone else. I can't let her do this. I can't let her put her life on the line for me."

Finn tried to go to Luisa—to stop her—but several pairs of strong hands dragged her back into her seat. And an almost imperceptible shake of Luisa's head held her there. Finn's heart lurched in her chest when Javier pointed his gun at Luisa's head. Her helmet looked sturdy, but could it stop a bullet at such close range? Finn didn't want to look, but she couldn't turn away.

"Where's Manuel?" Javier asked in Spanish.

"Counting your money," Luisa replied in kind. "One hundred million dollars is a lot of bills. That takes time. I'm sure he'll call you when he's done."

Finn didn't know which was sexier, hearing Luisa speak her native language or watching her stand up to the man who had been tormenting them for hours on end.

Javier cocked his head. "You're awful calm for someone who's about to die a slow, painful death. You've got a large set of balls on you, Moreno."

"Is that why your grandmother tried to hook us up, so I could show you how to grow a pair?"

A corner of Luisa's mouth quirked up into an insouciant smile that charmed Finn but enraged Javier. He roared in anger and backhanded Luisa across the face. The butt of his gun struck her on her cheek, opening up a sizable cut on the right side of her face. Her helmet went flying, and her goggles skittered across the hardwood floor. Blood poured down her cheek, but she didn't wipe it away. She kept her eyes on Javier. Watching him. Waiting for his next move. And, Finn hoped, planning her own.

"Is she trying to piss him off?" Katie asked.

"If she is," Finn said, "she's doing a hell of a good job."

"You got everything you asked for," Luisa said as a rivulet of blood dripped down the side of her neck and seeped into the collar of her uniform. "Let the hostages go."

After the Spanish speakers in the room translated the conversation for those who didn't understand or couldn't hear what was being said, an excited buzz filled the air at the prospect of freedom. But Javier quickly dashed everyone's nascent hopes.

"I can't let them go yet. I want them to witness your

execution first. That's a vacation memory that should last a lifetime, don't you think?" He forced Luisa to her knees and pressed the gun to the back of her head. "Do you have any last words before I do what my grandmother couldn't?"

"Just one."

Luisa scanned the crowd, her eyes taking in the sea of faces staring back at her. Then she turned her eyes toward Finn, her gaze as warm and tender as a caress.

"Now."

A single gunshot rang out as the room went dark. In addition to frightened screams, Finn heard the distinctive chop of helicopter rotors, a jumble of voices yelling commands, and the staccato bursts of automatic gunfire.

She threw herself on the floor and wrapped her arms around her head. Others near her did the same. She assumed Jill and Ryan were curled up next to her, but she couldn't see anything in the inky darkness that enveloped them.

All around the room, bullets ricocheted off hard surfaces or thumped into soft ones. Finn heard screams of fear, cries of pain, and the thud of bodies hitting the floor.

She started to crawl away—to feel her way in the dark until she reached the nearest exit—but she forced herself to remain where she was. She couldn't see well enough to avoid getting caught in the crossfire.

So she closed her eyes and waited for it to be over. She waited for her nightmare to finally come to an end.

❖

Luisa didn't take time to think. As soon as she gave the signal to her colleagues monitoring the feed from the hidden camera, she pitched forward and rolled to her left. She felt the bullet from Javier's gun graze her shoulder. The missile tore through her uniform shirt and seared her flesh, but as far as she could tell, didn't pierce her skin.

She scrabbled on the floor like a crab, blindly sweeping her arms across the terrain in front of her. Her left hand struck what felt like her helmet. She started to put it on, but the chin strap was too damaged to keep it in place so she tossed it aside and kept searching for what she really needed—her night vision goggles. She nearly cried with relief when the fingers of her right hand slid across one of the polycarbonate lenses.

She placed the goggles over her eyes and cinched the adjustable strap to secure them into place. The room that had been pitch-black seconds before now glowed neon green. She squinted to protect her eyes from the bright white flashes of muzzle fire as Javier's men and the Federal Police tried to gun each other down.

As she slowly scanned the room, she saw the hostages diving under their chairs to seek cover. She saw her colleagues rushing in to save them. And she saw Javier's men fighting to hold their ground. What she didn't see was what she wanted to see the most: Javier Villalobos. She pulled her pistol from its hiding place in the back of her waistband and joined the fray.

The vans Director Chavez had called for didn't contain the ransom Villalobos had demanded but reinforcements. When Manuel had opened the rear doors to inspect the cargo, he had been greeted not by the riches he had been expecting to see but twenty armed men drawing down on him. He had tried to turn and run, but Director Chavez had held him in place by draping a beefy arm across his shoulders.

"Act like everything's okay," Director Chavez had said, "or my men will kill you before you take two steps."

Manuel had nodded like a bobblehead doll and flashed a thumbs-up sign to his fellow gunmen.

"Good," Director Chavez had said. "Now pretend to search Officer Moreno for weapons and send her inside. Then climb into the van to 'count your loot.'"

Manuel had reluctantly acted as instructed. When he climbed in the van, an officer had taken his weapons, handcuffed him, and placed a muzzle over his mouth so he wouldn't be tempted to call out a warning to the rest of his fellow gunmen.

As Luisa walked toward the theater, she had heard a helicopter in the distance. Javier's men had probably thought the chopper was just another news crew covering the standoff, but she had known it contained the remaining members of her team. The ones who had lowered themselves to the roof of the theater and worked their way inside while the troops on the ground advanced on the gunmen outside.

The battle was fierce but brief. It lasted only a few minutes, but for the hostages, it probably felt like hours. After the command came to cease fire, the emergency lights were turned on, and Luisa removed her night vision goggles so she could inspect the damage.

The room was in shambles. Bullet holes pockmarked the ceiling, walls, and floor. Dozens of gunmen lay dead or dying. Others held their hands over their heads and pleaded for mercy. Some of the hostages were wounded, too, though none of the injuries appeared to be mortal. Thankfully. Luisa didn't want to imagine the fallout if one of the hostages had been killed by friendly fire. After Javier's men were ushered out and herded into the waiting vans, officers began ushering the hostages who could walk to safety and directed medical personnel to tend to the ones who couldn't.

Luisa tried to locate Finn in the chaos but didn't see her. Then she heard Finn yell her name. She turned toward the sound just in time to see Javier Villalobos using Finn as a human shield as he backed out of the room. Luisa drew down on him.

"Javier Villalobos, you're under arrest. Release your hostage, drop your weapon, and put your hands over your head."

"If you want me, Moreno, you have to come get me. Make it fast or your girlfriend and I will get this party started without you."

He kept going despite her admonitions for him to stop so she gave chase. Despite her desperate desire to apprehend him and free Finn, her pursuit was controlled rather than reckless. She slowly advanced toward him while he dragged Finn through a phalanx of officers helpless to halt his progress. They couldn't fire on him without risking hitting Finn—or causing the gun he was holding on her to accidentally discharge.

"Give it up, Villalobos," she said as she continued her steady pursuit. "It ends here."

"It ends when I say it does."

Luisa tightened her finger on the trigger of her gun but didn't squeeze. For an absurd moment, she wished she could be like a character in one of Angelina Jolie's action films. The one where Angelina and her crew of assassins had defied the laws of physics by getting bullets to curl instead of traveling in a straight line. If she could do that, she could save Finn from this madman once and for all. Instead, she watched helplessly as Villalobos backed toward the speedboat moored in the lagoon and climbed aboard.

Using a pair of plastic handcuffs he must have stolen from a fallen officer, Villalobos tried to bind Finn's wrists to the boat's railing. She resisted his efforts to restrain her, so he was able to tie only one of her hands, not both. As Finn tried in vain to free herself, Villalobos started the engine and gunned the throttle.

Luisa didn't hesitate. She holstered her gun, jumped into a second speedboat moored nearby, and went after him.

The boats' lights illuminated the dark lagoon as waves from the churning engines crashed against the shore. Luisa registered the rows of empty hotel rooms looming dark and abandoned on her left and right, but her main focus was on the boat in front of her. On the fleeing suspect behind the wheel and the woman he had forced to accompany him. She was determined to capture both. So she could put Javier Villalobos away for the rest of his life, and love Finn Chamberlain for the rest of hers.

"Fuck you, Moreno," Villalobos yelled, the words nearly drowned out by the wind whipping in Luisa's ears.

He stuck one arm out and fired off a series of wild shots. Luisa ducked behind the Plexiglas mounted in front of the steering wheel of the boat she was driving, all too aware the thin composite material she was hiding behind was designed to protect the boat's driver from nothing more serious than wind, rain, and the occasional low-flying bird. Where was her riot shield when she needed it?

As she began to gain ground on Villalobos, she heard Director Chavez yelling commands in the receiver wedged in her left ear.

"Let him go, Moreno. The navy can handle it from here."

Navy warships were waiting in the Caribbean, but they were so far offshore they wouldn't be able to scramble the smaller crafts on board in time to intercept Villalobos's speedboat. She had to catch him before he reached open water. If she didn't, he would be gone. He would be the most wanted man in Mexico, but thanks to the folk-hero status he would achieve with the rather large segment of society who deified criminals, he would have plenty of places to hide.

"No can do, sir."

"Are you refusing a direct order?"

"I won't give up my pursuit, sir." Luisa had always done everything her superiors had commanded her to do, but not this time. She couldn't give Javier Villalobos a chance to escape. Not when so much had already been lost. Not when so much was still at stake. "I want to finish the job Carlos Ramos didn't get a chance to."

Director Chavez was quiet for a moment. When he finally spoke, he sounded more like a proud father than an angry commanding officer.

"In that case, go get your man."

"Yes, sir."

Luisa opened up the throttle even more. As the boat picked up speed, she braced her legs to keep from falling over. The hull bounced over the roiling wake trailing behind Villalobos's boat. She felt like she was riding a Jet Ski each time the boat went airborne and crashed back to the surface of the water. She gripped the steering wheel as hard as she could, praying the boat wouldn't take on too much air and flip end over end.

Overhead, news and police helicopters followed the chase. Thanks to the bright spotlights playing across the water, Luisa could see a small island in the distance. If she could steer Villalobos toward it, she could pursue him on solid ground, buying time for the navy to back her up and decreasing his chances of getting away. But if she got too close to him, he might ram his boat into hers and both vehicles could capsize—if they didn't go up in a ball of flames first.

She had to take a chance. A calculated risk that, if it didn't pan out, could end up being the worst move she had ever made.

She reached for her gun and told herself not to miss.

She aimed low, trying to avoid a ricochet that could hit the gas tank. Or even worse, Finn. When she was sure she had the shot she wanted, she fired three times in rapid succession at the speedboat's motor. All three shots must have hit home because the boat's engine began to spew thick plumes of bluish-gray smoke.

Villalobos's boat started to lose speed. When the engine sputtered and died, the boat drifted to a stop. Luisa pulled up beside him, her gun still drawn.

"It's over, Villalobos. Let me see your hands," she ordered.

He turned toward her but didn't comply with her command.

"Don't make me kill you."

"All right. You got me."

Villalobos showed his hands. His left hand was empty, but his right still held a gun.

"Drop the weapon." Luisa slowly enunciated each word as she tightened her grip on her own pistol. "Toss your gun in the water and place your hands behind your head."

"Whatever you say, Officer."

Like a magician trying to distract his audience with sleight of hand, Villalobos raised his left hand as if he meant to surrender, then jabbed the right in Luisa's direction. The gun bucked in his hand. Luisa fired off a round of her own. Villalobos's head snapped back and his lifeless body fell onto the bow of the boat, but Luisa didn't get a chance to linger over the sight.

What felt like a sledgehammer hit her in the center of her chest. The impact knocked her off balance. She stumbled backward and fell overboard, her hands clawing at the air as she tried in vain to breathe.

She felt the water hit her in the back. Then she felt it surround her and swallow her whole. Her lungs burned, screaming for oxygen, but she was unable to fill them as she sank further and further into oblivion.

Her last thought was of Finn. Happy, smiling, and finally free.

❖

"Luisa!"

Finn watched helplessly as Luisa tumbled into the water and disappeared below the surface. One of the helicopters overhead shined a light on the spot where Luisa had gone under. Finn stared at the spot, waiting for Luisa to resurface, but Luisa didn't come up for air.

Finn tugged at the restraint around her wrist but couldn't pull herself free. Sliding her hand along the railing wasn't an option either. The handcuff was cinched too tight to allow freedom of movement. Growing desperate, she kicked open a nearby storage compartment and peered inside, looking for something—anything—she could use. She spotted a utility knife, stretched to reach it with her free hand, and flicked it open. She placed the serrated blade between her wrist and the restraint and sawed frantically at the reinforced plastic strap.

She could feel the minutes ticking away. Along with Luisa's chances of survival.

When the handcuff finally gave way, she tossed it aside and gathered her courage for what she knew she needed to do. She had never been especially fond of the open water and, thanks to an unpleasant encounter with a piranha in the muddy Amazon River, she absolutely loathed water she couldn't see through.

Refusing to let her fear get the best of her, she threw herself headfirst into the inky depths, diving lower and lower as she searched for the woman who had saved her life by risking her own.

The helicopter's spotlight penetrated only a few feet below the surface of the water. Finn opened her eyes wider, straining to see as the light began to fade. She spotted a shadow a few feet further down. Was it seaweed, a passing fish, the resort's resident stingray, or a hand reaching out for hers?

She lurched toward it, and her fingers brushed against Luisa's wrist. She latched on and pulled, kicking toward a surface that seemed much too far away.

Her heart, taxed by exertion, lack of oxygen, and fear, felt like it couldn't take much more. Neither could she. The uncertainty she had felt during the past twelve hours paled in comparison to the uncertainty she felt now, her concerns for her own safety dwarfed by her concerns for Luisa's well-being.

Finally, her head broke the surface. And she inhaled a lungful of the sweetest air she had ever tasted. She lay on her back and pulled Luisa on top of her, making sure to keep Luisa's head above the water. Then she backstroked toward the undamaged speedboat Luisa had piloted. She was too tired and weak from her desperate dive to drag Luisa out of the water and into the boat itself, so she maneuvered Luisa's limp body onto the small ledge on the back and tried to determine how badly she was wounded.

She had seen Javier take aim. She had watched as his shot had hit Luisa squarely in the chest. Had the bullet ripped through her heart, or had she been lucky enough to escape with only a flesh wound?

Finn felt something cold and hard when she tore at Luisa's body armor. She tugged at the object and peered at a badly misshapen hollow point bullet. Figuring the police might need the bullet as evidence—or Luisa might want to keep it as a macabre souvenir—she shoved it in the back pocket of her sodden cargo shorts. Then she pulled off Luisa's body armor, tossed it aside, and shoved her hand inside Luisa's uniform shirt, feeling for blood. Her fingers came away clean, but

Luisa's chest was eerily still. Luisa's body armor had prevented the bullet from penetrating her skin, but the force of the blow had stopped her heart.

Finn pulled herself up on the narrow ledge and straddled Luisa's body.

"Come on, super cop," she said as she placed her hands on Luisa's chest and began gentle but forceful compressions. "Breathe."

She pinched Luisa's nostrils shut, placed her mouth over hers, and forced air into her lungs. Then she sat back, waiting for Luisa's chest to rise and fall on its own. Detecting no movement, she repeated the process. Again. And again. And again.

Finn tossed her hair out of her face, wondering if the salty liquid running down her face was seawater or tears. She caressed Luisa's cheek, certain of the answer.

"We were supposed to tell each other all our secrets, not part ways with so many things left unsaid. This is not how this was supposed to end."

Luisa coughed wetly, her shoulders bouncing with effort as her body tried to convince itself it was no longer drowning. She turned toward Finn with a faint smile on her face.

"Did you have something better in mind?" she asked, her voice raspy.

"As a matter of fact, I do."

Finn's tension melted away, replaced by an almost overwhelming sense of contentment. She didn't feel aimless anymore. She was meant to be here. With this woman. Now. And forever. She kissed Luisa. Feeling the life flow back into her. Feeling it flow into herself.

"I don't know about you," she said, "but I could use a vacation."

"I know the perfect spot."

Luisa opened her arms, inviting Finn to return to the best place she had ever been. The place she never intended to leave.

Finn placed her head on Luisa's chest and listened to her heart beat as they waited for help to arrive. She had listened to bagpipers in Scotland, the Vienna Boys Choir in Austria, and an impromptu concert given by a trio of goat herders in the Maldives, but she had never heard such a beautiful sound.

"What word did you pick up from this trip?" Luisa asked wearily.

Finn could barely hear her over the sound of the rotors overhead.

"What?"

Luisa stroked Finn's hair. Her hands were cold and wrinkled from the time she had spent in the water, but Finn didn't mind. In fact, she had never felt so comforted. So safe. So loved.

"When we met, I said you must have picked up a lot of souvenirs over the years, but you said the only thing you like to bring back from a trip is a word deeply ingrained in the culture you've just visited but has no counterpart in English. What word did you pick up from my culture that has no counterpart in yours?"

Finn thought for a moment. But only a moment because she didn't need a great deal of time to come up with the answer.

"Acceptance."

"What do you mean?"

"I've always felt like people were judging me when it was often the other way around. I needed to learn to give people a chance to be accepting instead of assuming they wouldn't and keeping part of my life—part of myself—secret from them. I learned how to do that this week." The women of SOS Tours had accepted her without question. She had not only made several new friends. She had made a change. A change she hadn't seen coming, though she welcomed its arrival. "I learned something else, too."

"What's that?"

Finn lifted her head so she could look Luisa in the eye. "I love you, super cop."

Luisa kissed her. "I love you, too, *mariposa*."

Finn grinned. The nickname could have held negative connotations for her because it was the same name as the hotel where she had just spent the worst night of her life, but her heart soared when she heard Luisa say it. Because now the name truly seemed to fit. She felt like a butterfly emerging from a chrysalis. Thanks to the events of the past week, she would never be the same again. And she would never be alone.

Because no matter where she went, Luisa Moreno would always be by her side. And in her heart.

Vacation Stretcher

Luisa held Finn's hand as they walked across the gangplank that led to the waiting cruise ship. Over a thousand other women—some in couples, some traveling in groups or on their own—had also gathered to make the journey.

To make up for the traumatic experience their guests had endured in Cancún, the management of SOS Tours had offered them free vacation vouchers for a trip for two to the destination of their choice. Understandably reluctant to take a chance on another resort trip, Finn had chosen to use her vouchers on a cruise from Fort Lauderdale, Florida, to Half Moon Cay, Bahamas, with stops in Grand Turk, Turks and Caicos, and San Juan, Puerto Rico, along the way. Now she and Luisa were cashing it in.

Luisa couldn't wait to have some fun in the sun with Finn, along with all the umbrella drinks and overflowing buffets they could handle. They hadn't had any real downtime since the incident at the Mariposa Resort. They had taken a few days off after the case was closed and before Finn returned to America, but neither had been able to completely put recent events out of her mind. Their time together had been spent recovering and reconnecting. Now it was time to start moving forward. To start building a future. What better way to do that than on vacation? When they could relax and be themselves without having to worry about deadline pressure or backlogged cases.

Luisa had been on a ship before, if a day trip on a casino boat to celebrate her cousin's thirtieth birthday counted, but she had never been on a cruise before. And she had definitely never taken a trip with so many glamorous stops along the route. Her family's idea of vacation was packing up the car and driving to a relative's house for a few days or spending a long weekend at the beach. With Finn in her life, however, she knew some things were about to change.

Some things already had.

She still loved her job and was as dedicated to eradicating crime as she ever was, but she didn't take the same risks she used to take when she first joined the force. She couldn't afford to be as reckless as she once was now that she had someone to come home to. Technically. She and Finn didn't live in the same city yet, but that was just a matter of time. She knew they would end up together. The only question was where. Mexico City? Dallas? Cancún? San Francisco? Perhaps they should throw a dart at a map and make a life wherever it landed. Because it didn't matter where they ended up as long as they were together.

"What do you want to do first?" Finn asked after a steward showed them to their room, a small cabin just above the water line.

Luisa turned away from the view of the pier outside the porthole window and steered Finn toward the bed.

"I can think of one thing."

"We have eight days and seven nights for that," Finn said with a playful grin. "Why don't we unpack our bags and take a look around the ship so we can get our bearings before the kick-off concert starts? We'll need to decorate our door at some point, but that can wait until tomorrow. After we find out where everything is and see how many of our friends are on board, we can spend the rest of the afternoon in bed."

The social anxiety Finn had struggled with for so long finally seemed to be a thing of the past. She made friends easily, primarily because she had learned to let people in instead of holding them at arm's length. People gravitated to her. And rightfully so. She was smart, funny, and filled with dozens of stories culled from her travels around the world. Who could resist her?

Luisa loved seeing Finn like this: engaged and happy. At the moment, though, she wanted to see her in a much different way: naked and wanting.

"There's no time like the present, I always say."

She pulled the suitcase from Finn's hand and let it fall to the carpeted floor. Then she pushed Finn onto the bed, lay on top of her, and claimed her lips in a kiss. She didn't want to see the ship. Not when everything she wanted to explore was right here in this room. Finn evidently felt the same way. She moaned deep in her throat and rubbed the sole of her foot against the back of Luisa's leg.

"I like the way you think, super cop."

"And I like the way you feel." Luisa pulled Finn's Intellectual Badass T-shirt over her head and ran a hand over the exposed skin. "Though I sometimes question your taste in fashion accessories."

A spent bullet hung from a chain around Finn's neck. Luisa fingered the misshapen projectile that had almost taken her life.

"Why did you keep it?" she asked.

"I wanted something to remember you by."

"No, really."

Finn covered her hand with hers. "Maybe I wanted something to remind me how close I once came to losing you."

"You almost lost me," Luisa said, "but you also brought me back." She still had the occasional nightmare about the night she had helped to bring Javier Villalobos and the rest of the Jaguars down, but the bad memories were more than offset by the good ones she was creating with Finn. "Now you're stuck with me."

Finn smiled. "That works both ways, you know."

Luisa caressed Finn's cheek as the ship's horn sounded and the massive craft slowly pulled away from shore. "I can live with that if you can."

Finn smiled up at her. "If I have to."

Luisa kissed her again. She sighed when Finn unbuttoned her shirt and slid her hands across her skin. Whenever Finn touched her, it always felt like the first time. Yet each time was better than the last.

She unbuckled Finn's bra and cupped her breasts in her hands. Finn arched her back, rising to meet her.

"Okay," Finn said, pulling her closer, "maybe sightseeing can wait an hour."

Luisa grazed her teeth along the side of Finn's neck.

"Just one hour? Are you sure that's going to be long enough?"

Finn hissed with pleasure when Luisa gently pinched her nipples.

"Okay, maybe two."

Finn flipped Luisa onto her back and finished undressing her. Luisa loved the constant shift in power between them. Neither of them ever had the upper hand for long. Unless, of course, that hand was doing something that felt incredibly good at the time.

"Stop looking at the clock." To help her cause, Luisa pulled off Finn's glasses and set them on the utilitarian nightstand next to the bed. "You're on vacation. For real this time, not for the sake of a column. Toss the itinerary out the window. There's nothing we have to do for the next few hours except enjoy each other's company. This week, we have all the time in the world."

"And after that," Finn said dreamily as Luisa rubbed her sides, "we'll have the rest of our lives."

"I like the sound of that."

Luisa pulled Finn toward her. Before she could lose herself in the woman she had fallen for practically from the moment they met five months ago, she heard a familiar popping sound in the distance.

"Are those fireworks?" Finn asked warily.

"No." Luisa reluctantly pushed Finn off her and reached for her clothes. "Gunshots."

Finn's expression bore a trace of unwanted déjà vu.

"Here we go again."

About the Author

Yolanda Wallace is not a professional writer, but she plays one in her spare time. Her love of travel and adventure has helped her pen ten globe-spanning novels, including the Lambda Award–winning *Month of Sundays*. Her short stories have appeared in multiple anthologies including *Romantic Interludes 2: Secrets* and *Women of the Dark Streets*. She and her partner live in beautiful coastal Georgia, where they are parents to three children of the four-legged variety.

Books Available From Bold Strokes Books

24/7 by Yolanda Wallace. When the trip of a lifetime becomes a pitched battle between life and death, will anyone survive? (978-1-62639-619-7)

A Return to Arms by Sheree Greer. When a police shooting makes national headlines, activists Folami and Toya struggle to balance their relationship and political allegiances, a struggle intensified after a fiery young artist enters their lives. (978-1-62639-681-4)

After the Fire by Emily Smith. Paramedic Connor Haus is convinced her time for love has come and gone, but when firefighter Logan Curtis comes into town, she learns it may not be too late after all. (978-1-62639-652-4)

Fortunate Sum by M. Ullrich. Financial advisor Catherine Carter lives a calculated life, but after a collision with spunky Imogene Harris (her latest client) and unsolicited predictions, Catherine finds herself facing an unexpected variable: Love. (978-1-62639-530-5)

Dian's Ghost by Justine Saracen. The road to genocide is paved with good intentions. (978-1-62639-594-7)

Soul to Keep by Rebekah Weatherspoon. What won't a vampire do for love… (978-1-62639-616-6)

When I Knew You by KE Payne. Eight letters, three friends, two lovers, one secret. Can the past ever be forgiven? (978-1-62639-562-6)

Wild Shores by Radclyffe. Can two women on opposite sides of an oil spill find a way to save both a wildlife sanctuary and their hearts? (978-1-62639-645-6)

Love on Tap by Karis Walsh. Beer and romance are brewing for Tace Lomond when archaeologist Berit Katsaros comes into her life. (978-1-62639-564-0)

Whirlwind Romance by Kris Bryant. Will chasing the girl break Tristan's heart or give her something she's never had before? (978-1-62639-581-7)

Love on the Red Rocks by Lisa Moreau. An unexpected romance at a lesbian resort forces Malley to face her greatest fears when she must choose between playing it safe or taking a chance at true happiness. (978-1-62639-660-9)

Tracker and the Spy by D. Jackson Leigh. There are lessons for all when Captain Tanisha is assigned untried pyro Kyle and a lovesick dragon horse for a mission to track the leader of a dangerous cult. (978-1-62639-448-3)

Whiskey Sunrise by Missouri Vaun. Culture and religion collide when Lovey Porter, daughter of a local Baptist minister, falls for the handsome thrill-seeking moonshine runner, Royal Duval. (978-1-62639-519-0)

Dyre: By Moon's Light by Rachel E. Bailey. A young werewolf, Des, guards the aging leader of all the Packs: the Dyre. Stable employment—nice work, if you can get it…at least until silver bullets start to fly. (978-1-62639-662-3)

Fragile Wings by Rebecca S. Buck. In Roaring Twenties London, can Evelyn Hopkins find love with Jos Singleton or will the scars of the Great War crush her dreams? (978-1-62639-546-6)

Live and Love Again by Jan Gayle. Jessica Whitney could be Sarah Jarret's second chance at love, but their differences and Sarah's grief continue to come between their budding relationship. (978-1-62639-517-6)

Starstruck by Lesley Davis. Actress Cassidy Hayes and writer Aiden Darrow find out the hard way not all life-threatening drama is confined to the TV screen or the pages of a manuscript. (978-1-62639-523-7)

Stealing Sunshine by Tina Michele. Under the Central Florida sun, two women struggle between fear and love as a dangerous plot of deception and revenge threatens to steal priceless art and lives. (978-1-62639-445-2)

The Fifth Gospel by Michelle Grubb. Hiding a Vatican secret is dangerous—sharing the secret suicidal—can Felicity survive a perilous book tour, and will her PR specialist, Anna, be there when it's all over? (978-1-62639-447-6)